Riley P**i**ne the con**t**e**mp**or **an** ces of two contemp **or a** ry romanc **e** as you've never seen them befo **r**. Expect delicious, dirty and scandalous swoons. To stay up to date with all things Riley Pine head on over to rileypine.com, for newsletters, book details and more!

If you liked *My Royal Hook-Up*
look for other titles in Riley Pine's
Arrogant Heirs miniseries

My Royal Temptation
My Royal Sin

Or why not try

Sins of the Flesh by J. Margot Critch
Hard Deal by Stefanie London
Legal Passion by Lisa Childs

Discover more at millsandboon.co.uk

MY ROYAL HOOK-UP

RILEY PINE

MILLS & BOON

First Published in Great Britain 2018
by Mills & Boon, an imprint of HarperCollins*Publishers*
1 London Bridge Street, London, SE1 9GF

© 2018 Riley Pine

ISBN: 978-0-263-93232-4

MIX
Paper from
responsible sources
FSC® C007454

This book is produced from independently certified FSC™ paper
to ensure responsible forest management.
For more information visit www.harpercollins.co.uk/green.

Printed and bound in Spain
by CPI, Barcelona

CHAPTER ONE

Damien

I SWIRL THE amber liquid in my crystal rocks glass. Inside the club, I can hear corks popping and the sound of raucous applause, which means Marius, owner of the Veil, has just replayed the end of the Nightgardin Rally. Again.

I shake my head. He doesn't need to keep kissing my ass. I've already bought out the VIP room for the night, spending my winnings like they mean nothing. Because they never do.

Below my balcony, drunk revelers party in the street, all because I was reckless enough to use a hand-brake maneuver. One where the last racer to attempt it flipped his car and died before the pit crew could get to him.

I should be so lucky. Instead, here I am, strangers toasting me like I'm something so goddamned special, even while we all know the truth.

I'm a brother scorned. A prince banished. A killer.

But for them, I'm just some larger-than-life entertainment—the reckless, rich playboy who drives too fast and throws enough money around to make sure the party and the ride never stop.

"Your Highness? Marius has asked me to see to it that you are well taken care of. Can I get you another drink? Perhaps something to eat? Or maybe—a companion for the evening?" A voice beckons from the balcony door, but I don't turn to face whoever has the balls to address me like that.

Your Highness.

Nobody calls me that anymore, not because of any request I've made but because everyone the world over knows that an Edenvale prince in exile retains no such rank or respect, especially here in Nightgardin—a country my father and brothers consider enemy territory—which means this asshole is mocking me.

I hold up my barely touched glass of scotch, my back still to him, and assume this will be enough for him to leave me to "celebrate" alone.

Instead, the scuff of his shoe alerts me he's done exactly the opposite.

So I paint on my devil-may-care grin and turn to face him.

"Party's inside. I'm good," I say, taking pains not to speak through gritted teeth.

The man is dark-haired with tanned skin, dressed in finery unlike any of Marius's other VIP room employees—a dark tailored suit, gold cuff links, Italian leather loafers. I may face him in jeans and a button-down with the sleeves rolled past the tattoos on my forearms, but that doesn't mean I've forgotten the apparel I grew up in—the clothing I see my brother Nikolai wearing every time the likeness of Edenvale's soon-to-be king is splashed across a magazine cover or television screen.

"Very well, Highness. But should you need anything at all, I am at your service."

He grins, and a gold-covered canine catches the glint of the setting sun.

"Thank Marius for his concern, but the only thing I need is to be left alone."

The man bows his head and then says nothing else as he disappears into the club.

The only thing that truly concerns Marius is that I throw my money around his club again in the future, but having his crony call me Highness? That is pushing things a bit too far.

I drain the rest of my drink and slip inside the crowded room. No one takes note as I make my way to the rear staircase. They're here for the free party, not me. I head to the main level and the back entrance, the one that leads to the alley where my red Alfa Romeo—the race-winning vehicle—is parked and waiting for me.

And apparently, there's no such thing as fucking privacy tonight, because my car doesn't wait for me alone. Leaning against the brick wall of the club is a brunette beauty—Botticelli curls falling past her exposed shoulders to where her breasts threaten to spill over the top of her tight strapless minidress. A silver stiletto dangles from an index finger, its heel broken. In her other hand is a tumbler filled with a clear liquid. For a brief few seconds, I'm entranced, unable to look away. Then I remind myself that any woman who holds my attention for longer than that is trouble, so I shake myself free of her spell and storm to my car.

I reach for my keys, echoes of *Your Highness* ringing in my ears. I need to get out of here and clear my head.

But I'm fool enough to look back, and that's when I notice her bloodied knee.

Shit.

"Do you need help?" I practically growl as I stalk toward her.

She startles, sucking in a breath, then all at once regains a composure that is as practiced as my own reckless veneer.

"I think I can handle a broken shoe," she says flatly.

As I approach, though—because dammit I can't leave her like that—I note the scrapes on her palm as well.

She shrugs. "At least I saved the drink."

When we're face-to-face I tower over her, even with one of her four-inch heels still on. Her other foot balances on the tips of bare toes, the nails painted pale pink. I drag my gaze up her lithe frame to her heaving chest, glossy lips and dark eyes. I nearly lose myself in their deep pools.

"What's in there?" I ask, nodding at the glass.

"Vodka soda."

"Good," I say, then tug at the dress's torn lining hanging in front of her barely parted thighs. My fingertips graze her soft skin, and she yelps as I tear the fabric free.

"What the hell are you doing?" she cries.

I don't answer as I dip the piece of her dress into

her drink, soaking it. Then I squat so I am eye to eye with her injured knee, one hand behind it to hold her steady. It's here that I catch a glimpse of lace just north of her exposed thighs.

She gasps as I press the alcohol-soaked fabric to her injury, but something tells me it's not from the sting.

The sight of a woman's panties I can ignore, but dammit if I can't smell her—tangy and sweet—and it's all I can do to keep my hand still when I want to slide it up to confirm what I already know—that this strange beauty is wet behind that pretty pink lace.

"I don't get out much," she says with measured control as I clean the wound. "Not used to shoes like this."

I look up, and she stares at me unapologetically. Those eyes are familiar, but I can't place them. I swear I'd remember if I met someone like her before.

"Do you need a ride home?" I ask.

She glances toward the Alfa Romeo and then at me, those innocent lips parting into a wicked grin. Then she reaches for the hand behind her knee, slides it up between her thighs, confirming my suspicions.

"I thought you'd never ask."

Juliet

The Alfa Romeo purrs like a wild jaguar and handles like a dream along the steep road that is one heart-pounding hairpin turn after another. I trace my fingers over the stitching in the caramel-colored leather seat and admire the sleek Italian interior design.

"Where to?" Damien growls softly.

"I don't care," I tell him. "Please…just drive fast."

He acknowledges my request with a preoccupied shrug, and in a blink we're racing up the mountain at over a hundred and forty klicks. The world outside my passenger-side window dissolves into a dark blur, and it takes all my strength not to pinch myself.

Two thousand feet below, a random club-goer from The Veil is wearing my drab black gown and is two thousand Euros richer. My curves are crammed inside her handkerchief-sized dress. A reckless trade, but one I don't regret. It feels good to be a little wild.

When I hit puberty, Mother decreed that it was time to quit climbing trees and kicking around the football with the servant kids and start behaving like a Nightgardin princess…i.e: a stuffy, stuck-up, stick-in-the-butt.

The second I reached my sexual maturity, it was "bye-bye fun" and "hello monotony." I now get to wear clothing more befitting an elderly nun than a young woman of twenty-one.

I've been coached to walk in a demure shuffle, keeping my gaze downcast—especially if men were in the vicinity—while waiting for my marriage to be arranged. After that blessed event occurs, I'll be allowed the privilege of wedlock intercourse for the sole purpose of procreation so I may squeeze out a future heir and secure Nightgardin's ancient throne.

Let's face it…I'm a gilded goldfish destined to swim in useless circles until the day I get flushed down the proverbial drain.

The Alfa Romeo skids on loose gravel, wheels leaving the bitumen as I jerk forward, the seat belt catching between my breasts. My chest constricts.

A precipitous drop looms mere feet from the end of the hood.

My eyes widen. I recognize this place. It's Lovers' Leap. Once upon a time, centuries ago, two star-crossed lovers took their lives here, jumping to their doom. I don't know much about the legend's particulars. Mother, the queen regent, forbade my governesses to fill my head with what she deemed "silly romantic notions." Fewer novels and more nonfiction was her decree, preferably biographies about selfless women who sacrificed themselves for the good of their countries.

The man slouched in the driver's seat watches my every move with his enigmatic eyes.

Goose bumps prickle along my legs. When I think of his strong, calloused hand on the back of my knee as he tended to my wound, I go slick between my legs.

At last he speaks. "Got to say, it took me quite some time to place your pretty face, but it's finally come to me... Princess Juliet."

I can't hide my grimace.

"Not wearing your typical Nightgardin pillowcase tonight. That cocktail dress threw me off."

He reaches out and his big hand covers my bare knee, sliding up. Not far. Only a few inches, but it's enough to ignite a furnace under my skin.

He squeezes my flesh. Not hard, but enough that I tremble from a full-body shiver, my pulse quickening.

"Time to come clean. What's your agenda? Trying to start a goddamn war with Edenvale or what?" His laugh is bitter. "If so, lots of luck. Word on the street is that you're kept away from the media, so allow me to update you. My family despise me. See, I once killed a girl, one about as old as you, Princess."

"I know this," I hiss, knocking away his hand. "Do not think to patronize me, Prince Damien."

"Just Damien these days, doll. I was stripped of titles when banished." He idly rubs the dark scruff coating his chin. "But if you know that I'm dangerous, and that my beloved family has disowned me, why set me up to kidnap you and create a diplomatic row? Who's paying you?"

"Paying me?" I can't help it. I burst out laughing, and good Lord it feels good. At court, I must always remain so serious.

"Proper decorum is essential for a queen," Mother says.

But yesterday she added a second sentence. "And for a bride."

"I'm to be married." My laughter dies a quick death. "I'm not here to create a diplomatic scene. I'm here because palace maids gossip and I happen to have excellent hearing. They say that Damien Lorentz, the banished prince of Edenvale, can give a woman ultimate pleasure. Your talents and skill are legendary, even here across the border."

Now it's his turn to laugh. "Is that what they say?" he drawls. "I suppose I have seduced more than my fair share of servants."

"I've just learned that I am to wed Rupert Dingleworth, the Duke of Wartson."

"Insane." Damien furrows his brows in obvious disbelief. "That old goat's pushing sixty."

"Fifty-seven, but who's counting? Wartson submitted a specimen to the royal hospital, and the medical report makes it clear that he can still sire children."

"You've got to be joking." Damien sounds equal parts horrified and humored. "Are you telling me that he submitted his swimmers for genetic testing?"

I nod. "Marriage is for one reason in my world. Procreation."

"Fucking hell. What a tedious country."

"It's a matter of duty before pleasure. It's how we've endured for a thousand years." I flinch inwardly, hearing my sharp tone. I sound exactly like Mother.

"Fifty-seven," he says more to himself. "And how old are you? Eighteen?"

I make a face. "Twenty-one last week."

"Old enough for the Duke of Wartson to pump your womb full of his certified spunk?"

My flinch wipes the sarcastic smile from his lips.

"I'm sorry, Juliet," he says gruffly. "Your situation sucks. But I don't see where I fit in."

"I'm a virgin." I decide to cut right to the chase. "And as the future queen, I understand my obligations. But… I'll have an entire lifetime procreating with Rupert. All I am seeking is a way to survive the lonely years ahead." I lick my lips, suddenly shy. "A memory…a memory of one night experiencing absolute pleasure. And that's where you come in."

CHAPTER TWO

Damien

"Do you know the story of this place?" I ask her as we both stare straight ahead. The sun has set now, and before us lies nothing but a black abyss.

She shakes her head sheepishly, and I try to wrap my head around how sheltered this young woman truly is.

"Centuries ago, a Nightgardin prince—Maximus—fell ass over elbow for Calista, an Edenvale princess."

She scoffs. "You're so eloquent."

I shrug. "You didn't come to me for eloquence, Princess." She quiets, so I continue. "The princess was here with her father as the two kings tried to negotiate a peace treaty. Of course, no such thing happened. But when Maximus was charged with showing Calista the royal grounds while the two kings attempted to negotiate terms, it was love at first sight."

She snorts, and her hand immediately flies to her mouth as her pale cheeks grow pink.

I raise a brow, and she crosses her arms, defiant. It's a good look on her.

"Love at first sight? Please. Despite my future being mapped out for me without any say in the matter, I don't daydream about something better. About what could be. I'm not naive enough to believe in fairy tales."

I shrug. "Believe what you want, Highness. I don't need to finish the story."

She grabs my bare forearm, the tips of her fingers branding me with their heat.

"Please," she says. "Keep going."

I remove her hand from my skin and place it in her lap, needing the distance.

"I'm not looking to spend the next couple decades in a Nightgardin cell. But—as you wish. I will continue the tale." I take a steadying breath, wondering for a moment if she felt the same searing touch of her skin on mine. Then I shake my head, banishing the ridiculous notion, and continue. "When the kings emerged from the negotiation chamber, neither Maximus nor Calista was anywhere to be found. But the princess's lady in waiting was discovered bound to a tree in the woods, gagged so she could not call for help. She's the one who revealed that the young lovers had escaped on horseback hours before, riding up the winding path of this very mountain."

I watch her chest rise and fall, watch patches of pink flush the skin on her neck, her cheeks. The same hue as the panties I know she's got on under that tiny dress.

She swallows, and something about this moment and the silence—seeing the Princess of Nightgardin rapt from nothing other than my words—it's the most intimate thing I've experienced in a good, long while.

"They came—here?" she asks, her voice barely above a whisper.

I nod, one single, slow movement.

"Long before the roads were paved, this whole lookout was lush and green, the perfect spot for two young royals to…" She swallows again, and I hold off on giving her the satisfaction of knowing. Instead, I lean toward her, bold and reckless, my lips stopping short of grazing her earlobe. She smells sweet like vanilla, which makes me long to taste her. "And Princess," I whisper, "there is nothing like the joining of two people in pure, undiluted love."

Her breath catches—a tiny yet dangerous sound.

"Calista's lady in waiting led the palace guards and those the King of Edenvale brought with him right to this spot. It is said the king raised his own hand to his dishonored daughter, but Maximus put himself in harm's way instead. They didn't get a chance to plead for their lives. Swords were raised on either side, a declaration of war. Either way, they were already dead. So the two joined hands and backed away from the skirmish until no ground was left to tread."

I straighten and see a tear leak from the corner of the princess's eye.

"I will never have a love such as they did," she says, voice trembling.

I let out a bitter laugh. "You want a love that will send you to your grave? If that's the case, you're an even bigger fool than I thought."

She raises her hand, but I catch her wrist midslap.

"How dare you judge me?" she asks through gritted teeth. "You roam the continents taking anything and everything that your heart desires, yet I will never have such a luxury. Don't you get it? You may be banished, but you are free."

My grip tightens on her wrist, yet she does not struggle to free herself.

Everything my heart desires. What a fucking joke.

"My heart," I snap, "died in the wreck that killed the only person I was stupid enough to love. So don't you speak to me of freedom. I am a prisoner, just like you."

And if I give her what she came looking for tonight, I'll likely rot away in Nightgardin's highest-security prison—if the king doesn't kill me first. It would be reckless as hell to assume anything less.

But I stopped playing it safe the second I bedded my own brother's fiancée. I have nothing—nothing—left to lose.

"Are you refusing my request?" she asks, jutting out her chin.

I bait her. "What you're asking for is an act of treason. I may be a man without a country, but yours has tolerated my presence for some time now. It's the closest thing I have to a—" I bite my tongue before uttering the word *home*. I am not foolish enough to think I belong anywhere, let alone here. But an act against Nightgardin, even by a banished Edenvale prince, would put the rest of my family at risk. "I will need some sort of…insurance…that you won't have your way with me and then immediately report me. Or…if that is your endgame…at least something that will work in my defense in a Nightgardin court.

Though I doubt I'd even be given a trial." I'm mostly joking, because I know this night can end in only one way—with me behind bars and my family none the wiser. But she clears her throat.

"Very well," she says. "What do you truly know about Nightgardin law?"

I chuckle. "Enough that I understand a night with you could cost me my life, but I've already admitted as much. What are you playing at, Princess?"

She dips her head. "If they find out I lied—that I came to the city to consort with an Edenvale prince instead of cloistering myself in prayer—you will not be the only one guilty of treason."

My throat goes bone dry. "They would hang you in the palace square."

"Perhaps," she says. "Or worse. It would be justified. That would be up to the king and queen to decide."

It would be up to her parents to decide whether or not to kill their only child for the crime of fucking me.

"This is the only time in my life that I get to decide, Damien. Let me choose who gets to take the most precious gift I have to offer. Because I choose you."

She reaches beneath the skirt of her barely there dress and tugs her panties down her thighs, over her knees and ankles until they lie in a ball on the Alfa Romeo's floor.

My nostrils flare. There it is again, the faint tang of her sweet, intimate scent.

"No one knows I'm here," she says. "And by the time they find me, you'll be long gone."

She takes my palm, places it high on her thigh and simply says, *"Please."*

Somehow, with one hand, I maneuver the car into Reverse and onto the road as my other hand skims soft skin, sliding higher, until I'm there.

I dip one finger between her soft, wet folds, and she cries out, bucking in her seat.

"Fucking hell," I growl, then put the pedal to the floor, speeding off to certain death.

Juliet

I'm going to die.

No, really. I'll be dead before my next breath.

My back arches and my hips circle to an uninhibited rhythm.

Damien takes another hairpin turn, one-handed, because he's delved the other between my thighs. His palm dances over my clit, working me until my sensitive skin throbs in time with my pounding heart. When he plunges his fingers into my tight slit, the Alfa Romeo wheels aren't the only things squealing.

My whimper dwindles to a soft pant as I writhe, drenched with an unfamiliar need. Damien can't maintain expert control of this sports car and me all at the same time. It's too much. No man is this dexterous. He's going to drive us off a cliff to our doom.

But his long, relentless fingers plunge inside my folds, filling me up, taking me to the gates of Heaven. My front teeth clamp hard on my lower lip. I won't tell him to stop. Death might be close at hand—but by the old gods and new...mine shall be a glorious end.

"Jesus, doll. You're a hellcat, aren't you?" He does

that magic swirling trick with his fingers again, confident and in control, playing me like a virtuoso violinist, and my scream is a sound between a breathless yelp and a squeak of delight. My whole body begins to shudder. My derriere clenches as my thighs tremble.

Good lord, what is happening to me?

"Fuck, I love a woman who makes some noise while she comes," he growls.

Another perfectly aggressive stroke, and my inner walls pulse in a series of mind-blowing contractions that milk his fingers. When I grow still, he cups my sex and teases my silky strands with a soft tickle.

"You have a fucking amazing pussy," he growls.

But I'm too greedy for games, and too starved for touch.

"More." I grab his wrist and grind my pelvis against his palm without a shred of decorum. I can hear my wetness sucking against his rough skin and don't recognize this woman, wild and roused, filled with savage yearning. I've touched myself before. A couple awkward fumbles beneath my quilt in the dead of night, but I never knew exactly what I was doing.

It's humbling that Damien seems to know my body's responses better than I do.

"Shit," he snarls, slamming the brakes. We skid to a stop in the middle of the road. I turn around, tensing at the anticipated impact of another car, but the hour is late. No other vehicle is in sight.

"Climb aboard, love. But be a good girl and grab the bottle of lube in the glove box."

"Excuse me?" Climb aboard? Lube?

"Time to get your sweet ass out of that seat and straddle me. You want to fuck? Fine, but we're going to do it my way, Princess. And behind the wheel is my favorite position."

I blink once. Twice. But he says nothing, just regards me with those magnetic steely eyes.

Oh my god. He's not joking. I try to swallow. "Let me get this straight. You're planning to drive while having intercourse with me?" I grew up riding horses, but something tells me that losing my virginity to a man behind the wheel of an Italian sports car is nothing I could have possibly prepared for.

"Are you up for the challenge or not, Princess?" His eyes are dark as sin. "Because if the answer is no, I can turn this car around and take you back to the club."

"No! Wait!" I cry. "Don't do that." My hand trembles as I move to unbuckle my seat belt, nerves churning my stomach. But despite my unease, I want this; I want him—badly.

In for a penny, in for a pound.

"Hold up. One final thing." His voice is a warning, silk sliding over gravel. "Have you heard everything the maids said about my...prowess?"

"Just that you are an expert in the arts of love-making."

There is no humor in his chuckle. "And what do you think of my nickname?"

"Nickname?" I frown.

"The Backdoor Baron?" He sounds exasperated. "Ring any bells?"

My frown deepens. "I do not understand. You

are a baron? Weren't you stripped of all titles? And what's all this about a back door?"

His intense gaze threatens to undo me. "You really are a sheltered innocent, aren't you? The nickname is a joke, but not without an element of truth. I give women pleasure, but when I'm inside them, I only enter one way. Through the back door."

I wait for him to elaborate, but nothing is forthcoming. "You speak in riddles."

"Are you joking?" Two lines crease between his brows. "Isn't this why you sought me out? To have me give you pleasure while keeping your technical virginity intact for your husband?"

Confusion presses against my skull. Silently I curse my parents for keeping me so cloistered and ignorant of the world. And I curse myself for letting them.

He huffs a curt sigh. "All right, look. When I fuck, I don't do it here." He reaches under my dress and enfolds my sex. "I do it here." He slides his hand away and squeezes my backside.

Clarity hits me like a bolt of lightening.

Backside. Back door. Like…butt.

Oh!

My cheeks are surely turning the color of rubies. "People do that?"

"Sure." He winks. "They do with me."

"I…no…no… I do not want to try such a thing. I wanted… I mean… I expected…the front door?" I grimace. This conversation is by far and away the most awkward dialogue I've ever endured.

Beep! A loud horn breaks the quiet night, and a

Porsche swivels around us, the driver making a vulgar gesture as he passes.

"Right back at you, buddy." Damien hits the accelerator, resuming our journey. He quickly glances in my direction before looking back to the road. "I've met your betrothed, you know. The Duke of Wartson. We've played poker together once or twice."

"Oh?" The sudden change of topic confuses me.

"You really have to marry that horny old goat?"

Tears prickle in my eyes. "Indeed."

He's quiet a moment before breathing out a rough sigh. "Fine. I'll give you what you ask for. But not here. Not while I'm driving, and not in the back door. For you, I'm going to make an exception." His smile is rueful. "Consider it an early wedding present."

He drives slower, but just as masterfully. The perfect, chiseled lines of his face are made for brooding. I find myself hypnotized.

"Damien?" I ask at last. It's strange how his name tastes so familiar on my tongue. "Why do you only ever take women in the…back door? Have you never tried the, uh, front door either?" A mad sort of hope flickers in me. Perhaps I'm not so stupidly naive and innocent. Perhaps he is like me, a virgin.

That faint glimmer of hope is doused by his bitter chuckle.

"Yes, Princess. I've tried the front door. But only ever with one woman." His knuckles go bloodless on the steering wheel. "A woman who is now dead."

Realization dawns on me. "Your brother's fiancée. Your once future queen. You seduced her, didn't you?"

"Technically, Victoria seduced me," he rasped. "But I suppose I should be proud of my notoriety."

"She was your lover?"

"I had rather thought that she was my one true love." A shadow falls across his face. "But I was nothing but a boy, and it was all a lie. Yet when it came to our lovemaking…sex meant something with her. And I've never felt that way about another woman. So I still fuck. I just do it on terms that make it bearable."

My heart aches at the pain lacing his words.

We arrive at an exquisite hotel, and he pulls past the main entrance. Instead, we approach a gated drive from a side street. He punches a pass code into a keypad, and the great brass doors swing wide open. He pulls forward.

"So what makes me different?" I don't look at him. I focus my gaze on the ten-story hotel before us. I breathe a small sigh of relief that although we are in a public place, no one will see me enter. I don't want to be found out before I get what I came here for.

"I've been asking myself the same question," he mutters. "And I don't have a good reply. At least not an easy one. So why don't we go inside and see if the answer is hiding in your perfect pussy?"

CHAPTER THREE

Damien

WE RIDE THE elevator in silence. With any other woman, I'd have made her come at least twice before we reached the top. But something about Juliet is different, and it's more than knowing she is Nightgardin's virgin heir. I can't place my finger on it, but I want to take my time with her.

When we reach the hotel's penthouse, the doors slide open, and Juliet sucks in a breath.

Rich mahogany wood covers the floor that leads us to the main living space where the sofa—the color of the deepest ocean—sits before a roaring fire.

"How did you…?" she asks, and I grin.

"I tip well," I tease. "And in return, I get special—favors."

She blushes, then moves toward the couch, running her fingers across the lush fabric. She's barefoot now, having removed her one good shoe, and something about her seems so casual and comfortable in what must be the most foreign place she's ever been—a strange man's home.

I stride up behind her. "The only thing better than

Italian velvet against your skin, Highness…is me."
I brush a soft kiss on the nape of her neck, and she
shudders. Then she spins to face me.

"Damien?" she says, demure and shy.

"Princess?"

She licks her lips, then reaches behind and unzips
her dress. It drops to the floor.

"God in heaven," I say, my strangled voice un-
recognizable.

That same flush from before creeps up her neck
to her cheeks, and she grins. "Do you—like what
you see?"

I take my time drinking her in, ignoring my cock's
urgency to free itself from my jeans and plunge between those lithe legs.

Her full breasts are milk white, her pale pink nipples pebbling at their tips. Beneath the left one is a
constellation of birthmarks that, if connected, would
draw an arrow straight to her heart. I trace the shape
with my index finger.

"You should be allowed to love," I say, not knowing where the words are coming from.

Her breasts rise and fall as she breathes in and out.

"I will learn to love my husband," she says flatly.
"It is my duty."

I brush my thumb over her nipple, and she bucks
into my hand.

"I want to see you," she says, her voice barely
more than breath. "Before you do any more, I want
to see you while I still have my wits about me."

I nod, but because I am a greedy bastard, I dip
my head quickly and swirl my tongue around that
perfect, hardened peak.

She cries out, and I step away, grinning.

She narrows her eyes at me, then takes a bold step forward as she starts to unbutton my shirt. She opens it, running her palms over my chest, and pushes it off my shoulders until it falls to the floor.

Her hands skim over my biceps and my forearms. They slow as her fingers run over the raised scars I've made invisible beneath the ink.

She looks up at me, wide-eyed.

"There was a lot of shattered glass in the— accident." That last word tastes so bitter on my tongue I wish I could spit it out. Or take it back. Because I was behind the wheel. I was the one responsible for taking the life of another. Accident is far too kind a word for what I did. The Royal Police blamed the weather and absolved me of any technical crime. But I know the truth, as does my brother Nikolai, the man who loved Victoria too. If we hadn't run, she'd still be alive.

She reaches for my face, and I flinch. But she is not deterred. Her gentle hand traces my most visible scar, the one that runs from my left temple to the line of my jaw. The one no one ever talks about anymore because what is left to say? Every time I look in the mirror, I'm reminded of the monster I truly am.

"You punish yourself," she says.

"Stop," I tell her, but she shakes her head.

"Maybe you aren't as free as I thought you were. Maybe," she continues, unbuttoning my jeans, "we're more alike than I ever could have imagined."

I step out of my shoes and let her lower my pants and briefs to the floor. Then I step out of those as well.

"Oh!" she says, staring at my erection. Then, *"Oh."* This time with less shock and something more like reverence. "Can I...touch it?"

I chuckle, grateful for her act of levity, even if she didn't mean it.

"Here," I say, taking her hand and wrapping it around my shaft. I growl at the feel of her gripping me, and her mouth falls open in a perfect O.

"What now?" she asks, her voice cracking on the second word.

"Stroke it," I demand. "From the root all the way to the top, keeping the pressure firm."

She obeys, teasing me as she moves achingly slow until she reaches the tip, precome leaking onto my sensitive skin. As if she's done it a hundred times before, she swirls her thumb over my slick skin.

"Fucking hell, Princess," I grind out over gritted teeth. "Are you sure you haven't done this before?"

She lets out a nervous laugh, and her dark eyes meet mine. "It's instinct, I guess. And something about you makes me feel at ease." She slides down over my length and repeats the movement again. Then again. And Christ if I don't think my knees are about to buckle.

"Me?" I say, my voice rough. "I make you feel at ease? The monster of a prince who isn't even welcome in his own country? You want me to take the most precious gift you have to give?"

Because suddenly this isn't a game anymore. It's real. So fucking real my chest hurts. Because this woman deserves better than I could ever give.

Pleasure, yes. I have plenty of that in store. But

how can that be enough for her when she knows what her future holds beyond this night?

She tugs me toward her, and before I know what is happening, I'm between her legs, my tip stroking her folds as she sucks in a series of sharp breaths.

I groan. She's wet, warm and soft as silk. "What the fuck are you doing?"

She presses her chest to mine, squeezing my cock between her thighs.

"There's no such thing as love at first sight," she says, echoing her words from the Lovers' Leap. "Take me, Damien. However you want."

Before I can say anything in response, she tangles her fingers in my hair and pulls me to her, crushing her lips against mine.

You're right, Princess. There's no such thing.

Juliet

Damien feasts on me like a man possessed. Moaning, I surrender to his tongue's wicked assault, savoring each possessive glide. His mouth is everywhere as he treats my body like a triple-scoop chocolate fudge sundae with a cherry on top. I am reduced to making halting, mewling whimpers like a lost kitten.

My entire life I have felt alone, but in this moment, I am found.

"What happens next?" I gasp as he licks up the side of my belly. "You insert your penis in my vagina and we commence procreation?"

"Procreation?" he barks out a laugh. "Jesus, Princess. Imagine taking the Nightgardin throne with an Edenvale bastard in your belly."

I flush, reality returning for an unwelcome moment. "I'm sorry. Growing up I was never allowed to call sexual congress by any other word than procreation."

He stands and tilts my chin so I am staring up at him dead-on with no escape. No shame either. I'm utterly naked and at his mercy, and yet feel safer than I have in years.

"We're not having sexual congress either, my lady."

"No?" My voice is husky.

He shakes his head and leans in, his lips pressing to my ear, nipping my sensitive skin until an enticing heat spreads down my neck, radiating to my breasts. "This is the part where you say, 'Fuck me, Damien.'"

The word surges through my core like a jolt of electricity. "I… I don't say such things."

He smugly arches a single brow. "Too bad then. Because you don't get my cock unless you ask. No, scratch that. Unless you demand it. Because tonight's lesson is this…" He strokes the ruddy erection standing at attention between his muscular legs. "This isn't a penis. It's a cock. My cock. And I don't just put it in you."

I press my hip bones against him. "What…do you do?"

He feigns a solemn expression, but by now I know better. "Utter the secret password and you'll discover all."

"P-password?" I stumble.

"Fuck me, Damien."

I lick my dry lips and avert my gaze to his biceps,

perfectly sculpted and coursing with thick veins. Goose bumps pepper my skin as I mumble the words.

"I'm sorry," he replies coolly. "I didn't quite catch that."

I repeat myself a fraction louder, my hands balled against my sides.

He kisses me deeply, his tongue teasing mine in leisurely, long licks. "Still not quite hearing you."

I grab his chin and force him to look me straight in the eye. "Fuck me, Damien," I announce, loud and clear—so much so that I don't recognize my own voice. Because no such words would ever spill from my lips. Yet here they are. "Fuck me…hard?" I add the second part to my question on impulse, but it makes me achy and wet all the same.

He growls his approval. "Good girl."

He scoops me into his arms before I can draw another breath and carries me to a bedroom with an impressive king-size bed.

I expect him to toss me down and ravage my body like a depraved animal.

Instead, he eases me onto the mattress as if I am a rare and delicate gift.

"You are every inch a queen." A low rumble vibrates through his chest. His gaze full of dark promise…and something that I'd be tempted to describe as wonder.

Sweat mists my fevered skin as invisible flames fire through my belly. I know, I know, that I don't believe in love—especially with someone I just met—but at that moment, I swear I fall for him…just a little. Enough that I'm dizzy and giddy at the thought of his hands on me again.

"What do we do now?" I ask.

"Now I get some protection so we can fuck without doing any of that procreating you are all so fond of in this realm."

He turns and walks to his dresser, opening a top drawer. I admire his firm, masculine ass. I memorize the indents on either side of his buttocks and the way his hard quads bulge with muscle.

When he returns, he clutches a small silver square.

"How does the protection…work?" I grimace. But in this such case, I was never meant to be protected, for what queen would want protection from her king?

"Watch and learn." He rips the corner with his teeth and removes an object that I don't recognize. Then he places it on the edge of his…cock…and rolls it down.

"Oh, I understand!" I exclaim, catching on at last. "You are going to use that to catch all of the semen."

His laugh is no more than a single gruff bark, but nevertheless, it's genuine. "You're an odd little duck, you know that?"

I raise my chin. "No one addresses me like that." But then I drop the fake imperious routine and crack a grin. "All right, all right, you win. I am as odd a duck as there ever was. Sorry."

"No. Never apologize." His nostrils flare. "Your innocence, it's a rare thing this day and age."

"Perhaps, but I'd rather it wasn't my sole value."

Something flashes deep in his eyes. "I understand. And I'm not just turned on because you are a virgin. I… I…need you to know that."

I'm surprised. I never expected to see this notorious playboy seem uncertain.

"Here's the deal," he says. "I don't know what's happening here. But since I saw you in that alley, it's as if I've left the real world and entered some kind of dream." He crawls over me, tangling his hands in my hair. "Life suddenly feels brighter. I swear I smell roses and hear snippets of music. What the fuck are you doing to me, Princess?"

"This." I wrap my legs around his trim hips, and he presses right at the center of me, positioning himself at my wet, but tight, entrance.

"You're sure you want this?" He searches my face, and I do the same with him.

I know what he's really asking. Do you want me?

And god forgive me, I do. I really, really do.

He is so beautiful, scars and all. "I wanted you before I knew you. After all, you're very handsome," I admit shyly. "But now after meeting you... Damien. I need you. I need you to be the one."

He presses his forehead to mine, and as he gives me a deep, lush kiss, a shudder rocks him. "I don't know what the hell I've done in my shitty life to deserve you, but whatever it is, I'm grateful."

I laugh softly. "You promise you won't go for the, you know, back door?"

The corner of his mouth quirks into a roguish grin. "I am a man with sexual urges. I make no apologies for that," he says. "But I've only been inside one other pussy, and that was a long, long time ago."

"I imagine it's like riding a bike," I say, fighting for a levity that I do not feel.

His eyes darken as his tip parts my intimate lips. "Gorgeous, trust me. It's nothing like riding a bike."

And then, slowly, inexorably, he begins to enter me, inch by slow inch.

"Oh!" I gasp. There's a sharp bite of pain and then… "Oh." I moan. "Oh God."

He starts slow and gentle, sliding in to the root and then out again with such care it makes me ache.

Ache for him. For more.

"Christ, Princess," he says, sinking into me again, and I run my fingers over the taut muscles of his arms, his abdomen. And then I squeeze that perfectly sculpted ass.

It's glorious.

"I didn't know." My voice shakes. "I didn't know what I was giving up. And now that I do—"

He gives me a searing kiss before I can finish, and it's a good thing. Because if I spoke what I know now is the truth, I'd damn us both.

I don't ever want to give you up.

I'm being cared for. Revered. Worshipped. Damien slides a hand between my legs and works my sensitive pearl while filling me with every last perfect inch of him.

Sweat sheens our bellies. I can't be quiet. I try, but it's impossible. You might as well ask me to catch a rainbow between my fingertips. I buck and arch, my body moving like a wild thing that cannot—that from here on out will not—be tamed. I'm drenched and swollen with need. My inner thighs soaked with my own arousal, creamy for his granite erection.

He pulls me up and falls back on his knees, still joined to me and takes my breast into his mouth, sucking at my hardened peak in hot, confident pulls until I cry out, a sound so guttural I wouldn't know it was human if it hadn't come from my own lips.

"Fuck me, Damien," I whimper, and he raises his head, his eyes meeting mine, his gaze narrowed and intense.

"Louder," he orders.

"Fuck me!" I command, riding up then slamming down over him until he's filled me to my core.

He answers me with an animal roar, lifting me off the bed completely and pinning my ass against the wall, his cock still buried inside me, nestled against some hidden bundle of nerves.

He kisses me hard, and I bite his lip, tasting the coppery tang of blood. His thrusts come hard and fast, each expert stroke coaxing me to buck against him until my vision threatens to go black.

Then—I explode. I am a million pieces, every nerve so sensitive I fear the slightest touch now will bring me to tears. I'm not sure I'll ever be whole again.

I lower my legs to the floor, but Damien still holds me, as if he knows I might fall.

"Juliet." He whispers my name in my ear. "That was god damn beautiful."

His voice is full of the same wonder that courses through my veins.

I can tell it is with a groan of regret that he pulls from me, and I feel a flood between my thighs.

"Shit," he hisses.

"What happened?" I dip my head to see milky

white liquid running down my legs. "Have I done something wrong?"

He should be smiling, but his expression is grim. "No, gorgeous. You were perfect. More than perfect. But the condom broke."

CHAPTER FOUR

Damien

I SHOW A shaken Juliet to the bathroom, and she locks herself in. I press my palms to the door, my head falling against the heavy wood, and I hear the shower start.

"Fuck. What the hell have I done?"

I've most likely ruined the future queen of Nightgardin. I haven't set her up for banishment. I've put her on the path to execution.

Somehow I make my way to the edge of the bed where I sit, head in hands. Two women. I've only been with two women like this, and I've likely now sent both to their graves.

I hear the *click* of the bathroom door, but I don't dare move. How can I look her in the eye?

"Damien," she says softly, resting her warm palms on my bare thighs. "Damien, look at me. Please."

I lift my head, realizing the emotion that overwhelmed me when I was inside her was not merely from sex. Because at this moment I realize I'd do just about anything for this woman—this stranger whose life is forever changed because of me.

I expect her cheeks to be tear-soaked, the whites of her eyes to be bloodshot. Instead, I find a crystal-clear gaze coming from a woman I almost don't recognize.

"Juliet?" I ask like a fool. Of course it's her.

"Everything will be okay," she says with a sureness that makes my chest ache. Because she could not be more wrong.

She's wrapped in a plush white hotel towel, her rich brown locks dripping onto her shoulders.

"I fucked up," I say, cradling her cheeks in my hands. "Don't you see? This is who I am. I ruin anyone and anything I care about."

She grins and strokes my hair from my forehead.

"Are you saying you care about me, Damien Lorentz?" Then she lets the towel fall.

"What the hell are you doing?" I ask as her gaze falls to my cock, hard as a rock, my body betraying me.

"I am not fertile," she says. "At least, not right now. My governess taught me to chart my fertility the day I first bled. Orders from the king and queen. They wanted to be sure that as soon as I turned twenty-one and they handed me off to Nightgardin's next king that he would plant his heir in me on his first try." She grabs my cock, squeezes my shaft in her now-expert grip. "Of course I have not tested the method's effectiveness before tonight." She bats her long lashes at me.

My eyes widen. I've never heard of such a method, yet I've never given a shit what a woman did since what I did in the bedroom never put me in danger of getting a woman pregnant. How is she not afraid?

How is she not beating her fists against my chest, berating me for ruining her?

"I'm free of disease, if that's something you're worried about," I say, aiming to reassure her when the truth is that she doesn't seem the least bit nervous, and I wonder if it's not my own apprehension I'm trying to assuage. "I've always been safe with—" Saying it aloud now seems too boorish.

"With the countless other women you've taken from behind?"

Juliet finishes the thought, my bold little princess.

I nod. "Why is it different with you?" The question is more to myself, but something in me wants her to know that the second I buried myself inside her, everything changed.

"I don't know," she answers. "I sought you out for what I thought you could do for me physically." She kisses my forehead, her taut nipples brushing against my chest. My cock pulses in reaction. "But you were kind and caring the second you approached me outside the club."

"You were hurt," I say, curtly.

"And you could have left me to fend for myself. But you didn't."

She strokes my hair, her gaze unblinking and fixed on mine. Then kisses the tip of my scar at the side of my jaw, and my chest tightens. I've survived for years on the rush of fast cars and the types of encounters with women that allowed my heart to remain numb.

I rest my hands on her hips, my fingertips kneading her soft skin.

"I wasn't supposed to feel," I admit, realizing I'm

treading on very thin ice. Because feeling something for this woman is not an option.

"Do you want to know what I feel, Damien?" But she doesn't wait for me to respond. "I feel trust." She lifts my palm to her chest, my fingertips tracing the arrow of birthmarks, placing it over her heart—and her beautiful bare breast. "Right in here. And I feel safe."

I let out a bitter laugh. "You're deluding yourself, Princess. No one is safe with me." Of this I am certain.

She climbs over me, balancing so the tip of my cock teases her opening.

"If you could keep from hurting me, would you?"

"Yes," I admit with zero hesitation. "But we both know that isn't an option."

"This is, though," she says, sinking over me like a custom-made racing glove.

She gasps, and I growl.

"Juliet… Jesus… Do you not…understand…what just happened?" I can barely speak because I am inside her with no barrier, her rich, tight warmth driving me out of my goddamn mind. "If your little chart doesn't work, I could have put you at more risk than you ever anticipated."

She pushes my shoulders, urging me onto my back.

"I understand three things," she says. "The first is that it will take days for anyone to find me, as my governess believes I'm spending the weekend cloistered at the royal church praying and thanking God for the good fortune of my match."

This makes me grin. "You really are an evil genius in disguise. Do you know that?"

She raises a brow. "The second is that I'm not ready to give you up for my duties after only one night. Not yet."

I grip her hips tight and pulse inside her.

She writhes.

"And the third…" She pauses, and I watch that now-familiar flush creep up her chest, to her neck, and finally to her cheeks.

"Just say it, Princess. It can't be worse than asking me if we were going to procreate."

She lets out a nervous laugh, then leans down, pressing her breasts to my chest, her lips a breath away from my ear.

"The third is that when I do go home and marry Rupert, I'll have the memory of my short time with you—the closest I will ever get to being passionately, ass over elbow, in love."

I flip her over and kiss her with the hunger of a man starved of food, of water, of air, of anything and everything essential to the most basic survival.

Because she is all of these things and so much more. And so, for the next two days, I eat, drink and breathe nothing other than Juliet. I worship her body, and she nourishes my soul. She has unlocked a gate I thought no longer had a key, and hell if I know how the hell I'll ever close it back up.

On the morning of the third day, we languish atop my plush duvet. I pepper her skin with soft kisses from her ankles to her lush pink lips, then back down again. I pause mid journey for a quick taste of her tangy sweetness.

She gasps.

"I could survive on this alone," I say.

She laughs, pushing up on her elbows to look down at me. "You'd starve eventually."

"It would be worth it," I tell her, then give her one long, slow lick.

She fists the duvet, then collapses onto her back as she writhes against my lips.

"We're never leaving this room," she says.

"As you wish, Princess." And slip one finger inside her, then two, as I suck her swollen clit between my lips.

She bucks and thrashes, and I have no choice but to drive her the rest of the way home, taking immense pleasure in doing so.

"Damien!" she calls out as I do, and I realize there is no sound better than my name tearing from her lips.

I slide my hand free and crawl over her limp yet satiated frame, admiring the blissful smile spread across her face.

I put that there.

I lean down to kiss her, but before my lips reach hers, the bedroom door bursts open, wood splintering as six men rush into the room.

The Nightgardin Royal Guard, better known as the Black Watch.

Juliet screams as two of the men haul her from the bed. It takes the other four to restrain me. Even then, they're barely able to do it. My fight-or-flight reaction takes hold, and all I know is I will fight for this woman.

"Damien!" she screams, and I seethe as I watch her naked form being dragged toward the elevator.

"You fucking bastards," I hiss at my captors, but they say nothing. "Juliet!" I call after her, our eyes meeting as another waiting guard wraps her in a throw from the sofa. "I will come for you!"

She opens her mouth to respond, but one of the guards covers it with a less-than-gentle hand. She struggles against his grip. When the guard swears and snatches his hand away, I grin.

She's bitten him.

But my joy is short-lived, because they are in the elevator now, the doors already closing.

"Damien!" she cries one last time.

"I swear it, Juliet! I'll find you!" I yell just as the doors seal and she slips from view, and I know now that I was wrong. My name tearing from her lips in abject terror will haunt me for the rest of my life.

One of my captors punches me in the face before I can completely register that she's gone.

Then the truth of it all sinks in. They aren't just here to take Juliet to the king and queen of Nightgardin.

They're here to kill me, and there's not a goddamned thing I can do about it, not that there would be any point. I've committed an act of treason, one I knew was punishable by death. Yet I was fool enough to think that whatever connection Juliet and I forged would be stronger than the law.

Two of the guards pin my arms behind my back, but I no longer struggle as the two men before me trade punches in quick succession. A rib breaks.

Maybe two or three. One of my eyes swells shut, and a fist to the jaw makes me bite through my tongue.

My mouth fills with blood. None of the guards say a word as they continue what they were sent here to do. All the while I replay Juliet's screams in my head, the promise I made to come for her already broken.

Finally, my arms are freed, and I collapse to my knees. I cough, and blood sprays the floor.

One of the guards raises a rifle and aims the butt of it at my head.

"You better fucking kill me," I say, my voice thick and wet. "Otherwise I will be back, and I'll make every single one of you pay for what you did to your very own princess."

The guard with the gun laughs in my ruined face and whispers something in my ear. Then the entire world goes dark.

Juliet
Two months later

"Well, well, well," I mutter to myself. "Out of the frying pan and into the fire."

Outside the window, the towers and parapets of Edenvale Palace come into view. Across the blue moat rise huge statues of heroes and kings, marbled memories of past glories.

"Sorry, miss. I didn't catch that." The driver I hired at the border glances in the rearview mirror, tugging one side of his long, walrus-like mustache. I can tell he recognizes me but that he doesn't know from where. I have hidden my chocolate-brown waves under an Hermès scarf tied in a jaunty bow at my chin. My beige trench coat is expensive camel hair but unremarkable other than its elegant cut.

"I said, Goodness. Here we are." I set my hand on the small suitcase on the seat beside me. "Is the servants' entrance close?"

"Right around the corner, miss," he says before giving me another searching look. "Who is it you are going to visit again?"

"My cousin Dora," I lie. "She's been a maid at the royal court for five years."

"A Nightgardin maid? Working at the court?" he says, incredulous.

Blast! My accent has betrayed me in ways my hair never would.

I think fast. "Theodora, or Dora as we like to call her, was born in Rosegate." Rosegate is the disputed city between our two long-feuding kingdoms. "Right next door to me, in fact."

"Hmm, you're from Rosegate too, eh?" The driver clicks his tongue. But he hasn't called me out on the lie. He can't, because people from both of our kingdoms reside in that ancient town. "Well, miss. I do hope you enjoy your stay at the royal palace. Folks say it's gone a bit peculiar of late."

"Oh?" I try to sound interested, but not enough to attract attention. In reality, I am starving for any scrap of information about—

"Damien," the man says, finishing my thought. "The black sheep prince has returned from his years banished into the wilderness. Everyone is being quite tight-lipped about it. But my sister, Jenny, works in the kitchen, and she says that he has gone mad. I don't like speaking ill of the Lorentz family, God keep His Majesty, but that youngest boy was born as bad as they come."

Memories wash over me. Damien's confident yet gentle hands claiming my body, making me burn, making me his. In our stolen days together, it was as if we were placed in France's Large Hadron Collider, two particle beams thrust together at the speed of light. Of course the results were volatile. I was naive to have expected anything else. I see that now.

Damien was removed by Nightgardin guards as I was dragged away to my parents.

But…he said he would come for me. Swore it, even. Those were his last words as I was taken away.

He never came.

Perhaps the challenge seemed too great.

Perhaps I wasn't worth the effort to him.

The king and queen could have hanged me. Instead they hastened plans for the wedding—to tomorrow. So naturally, I ran away. Again. But this time I did not bother with any sort of lie. It wouldn't have mattered. I've been under lock and key ever since that weekend, every meal taken either with the king and queen or alone in my chamber. Each night my governess watched me place a sleeping tablet on my tongue—and each night when she left me, I retrieved the tablet from under my tongue and sent it down the toilet.

Last night when Elsie, the serving girl, brought my teapot, I asked that she join me. And because a servant cannot refuse a royal, Elsie drank a cup, but not before I distracted her and poured in two crushed sleeping tablets.

Soon after, I escaped out the window. No handsome prince climbed my tower and saved me. I did it myself.

My hand settles over my belly, still flat. No sign of the secret inside.

Maybe I fell fast and hard for a prince who fed me nothing but pretty lies full of tenderness and wonder, but now there is no choice. Our time together resulted in unexpected consequences. Ones he needs to answer for. Ones he needs to protect.

"Ah, here we are," the driver says, pulling up at the guard tower. "They'll fix you right up and give you palace security clearance."

"Thanks very much," I say, and slide out, tugging my suitcase with me.

Once I had a kingdom. Now I own two dresses, four pairs of underwear and a toothbrush.

But I'm free.

At the guard tower, the royal officer barely looks up from his newspaper. "State your business."

I untie the scarf from my hair and shake out my long locks. "I am Juliet de Estel, Princess of Nightgardin. And I demand an immediate audience with the Edenvale royal family."

The man's jaw nearly hits his ample belly. He clears his throat twice, his lips flapping soundlessly before managing to rasp "one moment, ma'am. I mean, miss. I mean, Your Eminence."

He doesn't pick up the phone beside him. Instead, he hits a red button on the wall.

"Yes?" A deep masculine voice says in a crisp accent.

"Mister X, sir, you're going to want to come to the

servants' entrance, right away. There's a…diplomatic situation unfolding here at the post."

Two minutes later a dark-haired man in a black suit appears, his eyes hidden by a pair of aviator sunglasses. He doesn't give me more than a passing glance before walking into the guard booth.

"The heir to the Nightgardin throne is at your post," he says.

"That's what I was trying to say. But more subtle-like," the guard replies.

The man removes his sunglasses and regards me with a look of cool appraisal. "Subtle indeed, Bartholomew. This is most unusual protocol for a state visit," he says.

"I'm a most unusual woman," I snap, refusing to be intimidated by his hooded gaze.

That earns me a ghost of a smile.

"Indeed."

"And since you know me, might I have the pleasure of an introduction?"

"I'm called X, Your Highness. Head of Edenvale's Royal Secret Service."

"X?" I chuckle. "X what?"

The guard Bartholomew joins in my humor. "That's what I always say. We have a running bet on what his real name might be."

"And it pains me to give you nothing but disappointment," X says wryly before reaching out to take my bag. "Will this be all?"

I nod.

"I need to speak with all members of the royal family… Prince Damien especially."

Something flickers in his enigmatic eyes. I get the

sense that this is a man who has seen it all and then some. I am the daughter of his kingdom's worst enemies, and he barely batted an eyelid. And yet when I say Damien's name I get a reaction that I'd almost be tempted to describe as sympathy.

"You're acquainted with Prince Damien?"

The strange way he says the prince's name sends a chill down my spine. I remember the driver's words. What has happened to Damien? The last I saw of him he was screaming that he'd find me–that he'd stop at nothing. Then two months of radio silence.

"He made me promises and broke them all," I announce. "And for my impetuousness, my mother ensured that I was broken in ways few can imagine. I didn't escape to rekindle a failed romance. I did it because a mother lets nothing—nothing—not solitary confinement, not interrogation, not hunger— stop her from protecting her child."

X's gaze follows my hand as again I lay a palm over my abdomen, as if the small gesture can protect the tiny spark inside. My now-solitary reason for existence, for having the courage, for risking everything.

"I see." And I can tell that in some strange way, this odd man does see. Relief sweeps through me as I feel protected for the first time since being ripped from that hotel room two months ago.

"Now take me to see him at once," I snap, recovering the royal imperiousness I wear as a second skin.

X's gives a curt nod. "Follow me, Your Highness. I'll assemble the royal family in the west wing."

CHAPTER FIVE

Damien

A SOFT KNOCK sounds on my door, and at first I ignore it. Despite having been home for a month now, the palace still feels foreign—like it isn't my home anymore. I guess had I not been left for dead in an alley behind the Royal Edenvale Hospital, I wouldn't have been welcome any time soon. The notion rankles, like lemon pressed to a long-festering wound.

Whoever is out there knocks again.

"What is it?" I shout with annoyance, then wince. My three broken ribs are healing, yet still tender.

When my intruder doesn't enter, I rise uneasily from the safety of the plush leather chair, put down my book and make for the door.

"What?" I ask, throwing the door open to find a tall, dark-haired man with a kind smile that makes my stomach turn. Not because I cannot stand his benevolence but because it's like looking into some sort of funhouse mirror—some semblance of the me I could have been had my life gone in any other direction but the one it has.

"Benedict," I say, greeting my older brother, the

one who gave up a life in the priesthood for Evangeline Vernazza, an artist from Rosegate. "To what do I owe this brotherly visit? Here to bring me another book? Or to tell me again that I need to give Nikolai time, that he'll eventually speak to me?"

I don't mean to spew my bitterness at Benedict. He's been nothing but concerned since they found me in the hospital—nothing but caring since I returned to the palace. But I doubt I'll ever prove myself worthy of Nikolai's forgiveness. And I can't say that I blame him.

Benedict sighs. "No pep talks today, brother." He looks me over and chuckles softly. "Forgive me for pointing out the obvious, but you've—looked better."

I run a finger down the scar from my temple to chin—the one from the car accident years ago. My beard bristles against my fingertips. I gingerly touch the bridge of my nose, but even that sends pain rocketing to my skull. When it didn't set correctly the first time, the doctors had to re-break it so I could breathe correctly again. Both my eyes are still rimmed with a mixture of purple and yellow. Then there's the new scar running the length of my right eyebrow.

This time I'm the one to laugh, a rare occurrence these days. My hand flies to my side, and I brace the other on the doorframe.

Benedict places a steadying palm on my shoulder.

"Are you okay?" he asks. "Should I ring the doctor?"

I straighten carefully and wave him off. "I'm fine," I say through gritted teeth.

My brother raises his brows. "You sure are going

to be a sight for bitter eyes," he says, and I detect a hint of amusement in his tone.

"What the hell are you talking about?" I ask.

Benedict throws an arm around my shoulder. "Join me in the west wing and you'll see."

I run a hand through my overgrown hair. "I was just starting a really riveting book. I think there are vampires in it. I really should finish it."

Benedict urges me out the door and pulls it shut behind me.

"To the west wing," he says again.

I glance at my attire—a falling-open robe, pajama bottoms and suede slippers—and shrug.

"Lead the way," I say.

Benedict walks slower than usual, making sure I keep up. Yet he's silent the whole way. Whatever waits for us at our destination, Benedict doesn't seem to want to tell me.

And for good reason. When we arrive, Benedict pushes open a large oak door that leads to a sitting room, yet no one inside is sitting.

Standing in an arc facing the door is my father, the king; my brother Nikolai and his wife, Kate, our soon-to-be king and queen; Benedict's new bride, Evangeline; and in the middle of them all, quite possibly the most beautiful woman I've ever seen, though I am still on some pretty heavy painkillers.

She gasps when she sees me, and I realize I must look even worse to those who do not see me on a daily basis.

"Damien," Nikolai says, the first time he's addressed me by name since I've been home. His voice is laced with disdain. He opens his mouth to finish whatever he wanted to say next, but the young woman rushes toward me.

"Oh my God!" she cries, then reaches a hand toward my face. I flinch, and she pulls away.

"What happened to you?" She pulls open my barely closed robe, spots the fading bruises over my ribs. "Damien. Tell me what's been going on for the past two months."

I stare at her, my brow furrowed. Then it clicks.

"Jesus," I say, my gaze shifting to Benedict, then my father and Nikolai. "What the hell is the Princess of Nightgardin doing in the Edenvale Palace? Are you all out of your minds?"

Nikolai crosses his arms. "So you do recognize her. Would you like to explain yourself?"

I let out a bitter laugh, trying to bite back the pain. But the princess's hand flies to her mouth. She notices my wince, and I hate that she is perceptive enough to register my weakness.

"Of course I recognize her. I have read a newspaper or two in my absence—even turned the TV to the news once or twice. Just because I don't—I mean didn't—live in my own country, it's not as if I abandoned all thoughts of home. I've kept up with what's been going on in our enemy nation. Yet now you've gone and invited the enemy into our home. Would you like to explain yourself?"

The princess rests a warm palm on my chest, and I raise a brow. Perhaps this day will prove quite interesting after all.

"Tell them, Damien. Tell them I'm not a liar."

"Tell them what, exactly?" I ask, amusement lacing my tone.

"About taking me home from the Veil. About our weekend in your Nightgardin penthouse." She rests her other hand over her abdomen. "About making love to me for three days straight, planting your seed inside me—and then never coming for me like you promised you would." Bitterness and hurt lace her tone as my head swims.

I back away, my hands in the air as if someone points a gun at me, which this woman might as well be doing because what she is suggesting could mean an all-out war.

"Slow down there, doll," I say. "I've seen you in the papers and on TV, but I've never met you before in my life, let alone planted my seed in you. What crazy fucking game are you playing?"

Her beautiful eyes fill with tears, but then she sniffs, straightens her shoulders and juts out her chin. "At least be man enough to say that weekend meant nothing to you instead of pretending like it never happened."

"Tell her, Your Highness."

I spin toward the door to find X standing right behind me, though I didn't hear him approach. He does shit like this all the time. He's not there...and then he is. To be honest, it freaks me the fuck out.

"Tell her," he says again, "how you lost the last year of your life."

Juliet

"Lost a year? What do you mean by that?" I snap, my voice husky with raw emotion. So much for my years of finishing school. All those tedious lessons on decorum and personal grace fly out the window. I'm reeling. It wasn't that I expected Damien to welcome me with open arms, be ready to parent our child and live a life beside me filled with sunshine, rainbows and unicorns as we danced cheek to cheek. But... I did harbor a mad secret hope.

At the very least, I expected him to express some basic human emotion upon seeing me, even if it was simply to be filled with regret over our ill-advised fling.

Never could I have expected that he'd disavow me altogether. The psychological blow is too much to take in my delicate condition. Sweat sheens my forehead as my stomach roils. Here it comes. A sickening sensation that is all too familiar of late. Oh no. Not now, I think, but like it or not, I'm going to be sick, and with no notice.

"Highness." X hands me a white paper bag, the same receptacle that one might find on a commercial airliner. I haven't the first clue how he procured it from thin air, but I am grateful nonetheless.

"Thank you," I reply as regally as possible. And then I empty out the contents of my stomach in front of an audience that includes not only my erstwhile lover but his entire family.

I am mired in one royal mess.

In the end, when my breakfast is folded up in the bag and taken away by a maid, I force my gaze to greet theirs. These faces are all as familiar as my own. My entire life I have been taught about our enemy to the south, how Edenvale has always competed with Nightgardin for wealth, land and reputation.

The bigger countries in Europe might chuckle at our border squabbles, but this animosity is no joke. It runs deep and cuts to the bone.

In Nightgardin, children are taught from the time that they are weaned from their mother's breast to never trust a citizen of Edenvale. Perhaps I should have been a better student.

"She is with child," X announces gravely. "And claims the child is Damien's."

The collective gasp fills the room.

Only Damien remains unmoved. "Bullshit," he drawls, tightening the bathrobe he wears. "That's impossible."

Prince Nikolai glances to him. "Is it, brother? I wasn't familiar you possessed so much…restraint… around beautiful young women."

Princess Kate places a warning hand on her husband's arm. "Darling. Deep breaths."

Damien lowers himself into a plushly upholstered chair and leans back, legs akimbo. "You're absolutely right, brother. I am a depraved, lust-filled monster. But I will still deny to my last breath that I could have fathered this child."

Benedict clears his throat. "Birth control isn't foolproof."

"Christ." Damien drags a hand through his thick, glossy black hair. The beard makes him look ever more the rogue, and yet I cannot deny my attraction. Damn this man.

"Thank you for Sexual Education 101, seminary dropout," he continues, and I wince at the way he treats his older brother. "But do you know what is foolproof? Not sticking my cock in a woman's honey."

"Dear Lord! That's why they call you the Backdoor Baron in Rosegate." Evangeline covers her mouth with her hand. "Heavens. I thought it meant you were shy and reclusive."

"And I could have lived another twenty years and never heard this story," the king mutters, face pale.

I fist my hands at my sides. "You made love to me the...old-fashioned way," I mumble, cheeks aflame. My parents had punished me with months of solitary confinement. But this moment is the worst I have endured. My humiliation is complete. All I have left is anger.

"Another lie, Highness. I don't make love," he snarls. "I'm told I can't even feel such a rarefied emotion, right, family?"

"Why are you doing this?" I shout, my pulse loud in my ears. "What's happened to you?"

X steps forward before Damien has a chance to respond. "Prince Damien was dumped at the royal hospital two months ago. As you can see from the wounds not yet healed, he'd been severely beaten. And he appears to suffer from amnesia concerning the days surrounding his misadventure."

I suck in a sharp breath and turn my gaze to Damien, now understanding the earlier comment. "I thought X said you'd lost the whole year."

He taps his temple with his index finger. "It's slowly returning as I heal," he says. "The last I remember now, I'd won the Nightgardin Rally. Not long after, my body was dumped at the hospital's service entrance. It all seems to add up. Except you, that is. I'd have remembered your pretty back door, and I guarantee you'd not be with child after such an encounter."

The king presses the heels of his palms to his eyes while I fight the urge to slap him silly.

"My mother's guards had you beaten for being with me. They weren't exactly gentle dragging you away."

"You're quite a storyteller, doll," he snaps in a harsh tone. "Most likely I racked up too many gambling debts."

I stride closer to where he lounges in the chair, looking this stranger up and down. I may remember our weekend together, but certainly do not know this Damien.

Ice and stone.

I didn't expect flowers and roses, but this is like being trapped in a waking nightmare.

"I don't know who you are, my prince. The man that I spent three magical days with was gentle and considerate." Exhaustion permeates my every pore, and before I can topple over, X positions a small stool behind me.

"How can we prove her story is true?" Nikolai asks as I sink down. His tone is not unkind.

"A paternity test will take time, especially if the pregnancy is only two months along," King Nikolai muses, stroking his clipped beard. "In the meantime, if we keep you here, your parents might well wage war to reclaim you."

I sigh heavily. "I know I have brought danger to all of you here, which should be reason enough to trust me. I would not risk so much for any other reason. But to carry a bastard in my belly, an Edenvale bastard at that—"

"No niece or nephew of mine will grow up with such a stain on their future," Benedict snaps with unusual feeling. "Brother, you will marry this woman today. Now in fact." He looks to me again, eyes wide with realization. "Were you not meant to marry the Duke of Wartson this week?"

I nod. "Tomorrow."

"Damien," Benedict says, his voice laced with dark warning.

"Never happening," Damien shoots back.

"I am not a priest, but I am a deacon in the Catholic Church, ordained to perform the sacrament of marriage. If what the princess says is true, and I sense no lie in her words, then this is how we can protect her, our own kingdom and the newest member of the royal family."

"I accept your proposal," I answer in a firm, clear voice. I like this brother. He is logical and ethical.

"His proposal." Damien is on his feet in an instant, but not without a grimace. I force myself not to feel sympathy for his injuries, not when he so clearly wants nothing to do with me and our child. "What about me?" he asks. "My say?"

Nikolai joins the fray. "You've put our family and country in danger." His tone is an arctic blast. "Marriage is the only honorable choice. Hell, Damien. It's the only safe choice. If the king and queen of Nightgardin find her before you right this wrong, do you think her intended will let bygones be bygones? They will execute her and your heir. And because of your…situation…in our court, I'm not sure we'll be able to protect you. But make her princess of both courts…"

"This is madness," the king says.

Prince Nikolai nods once. "But it is the only way." The king doesn't argue. "The Nightgardin court will hate it," Nikolai continues. "But their fury will be less than if we allow you to make a whore out of their only daughter and heir. Apologies," he says to me in a softer tone. "Those aren't my sentiments. Your kingdom is more conservative."

I clear my throat, rest a protective hand over my belly. "I understand. My own mother said all of your words to my face…and worse. She cursed the day I was brought into this world. She told me that she wished that I had never been born. It's only because Wartson never learned I'd been sullied that I am still alive—that the wedding is still on. But I obviously could not go through with it. Not with another man's child in my womb. Not with Edenvale's royal blood coursing through my child's veins. So I fled."

"How?" Damien narrows his eyes.

I shrug. "I tied four bedsheets together and escaped from my tower like any self-respecting princess. After slipping my servant girl a sleep aid, of course."

X steps forward again. "Sir, if I may," he says, addressing Damien. "Either you marry this remarkable woman, or I will."

Benedict and Nikolai chuckle, but Damien betrays no emotion.

I don't understand this family. Even in crisis there is humor here, and evidence of love.

"Do it not for her or even the child I believe will turn out to be yours," the king adds. "Because the worst possible scenario here is that you impregnated our enemy's heir, and face it, son. If there is a worst possible scenario, you will find a way to achieve it."

Damien winces at this, and despite the iron will I promised myself I'd have, my heart aches not for the wounds we all can see, but those he's kept buried far beneath his gruff surface.

I think about the possibilities if Damien and I marry, despite what he feels—or does not feel—for me. My child could grow up here and be safe. Have a life. Freedom. It's more than I ever could have expected with the duke.

And who knows, maybe the impossible can happen, and someday, far in the future, he or she will be able to bring an end to the tensions between our two kingdoms.

My gaze locks on Damien's, and this time I don't look away. It hurts to experience his stare without any feeling behind it—at least not the love I thought we shared. I should have known better, that I was not meant for true love. But at least here my child will have that chance.

Anger and suspicion surround Damien as an almost visible miasma. "Highness?" I ask. "What shall it be?"

This is not what I planned for my wedding day, but at least he is not an old lecherous duke. Never was this day a happy event in my mind, but I hadn't quite imagined the groom would be in his pajamas looking as if he'd just lost a bar brawl.

"What the hell? Let's do it," Damien growls. "But fair warning, Princess, I'm cursed." He winks.

I force a bitter grin. "Then it appears that we have very much in common."

CHAPTER SIX

Damien

"To the chapel, then!" Benedict says with a flourish.

I readjust my robe and tie it tight. There's being underdressed for an occasion and then there is flat-out ridiculous.

"He's wearing a robe, my love," Evangeline says, hooking her arm through Benedict's. Not that I expected her to come to my rescue, but thank fucking hell someone did.

Juliet unbuttons her camel-colored coat to reveal the servant's dress she wears beneath. It's a plain gray smock of a thing with a white apron tied over it. But something about the way her hair falls over her shoulders gives me a sense of déjà vu. I shake it off. There's no way that I would have made love to Nightgardin's princess as she claims I did. I was inside one woman like that, and I ruined her wholly and completely. What kind of fool would I have been to make such a mistake twice?

"We're quite the pair, are we not?" Juliet asks.

"It won't make the cover of *Vogue*." Kate giggles, then covers her mouth. "I think it's perfect," she says when she regains control. "You'll both remember your wedding day for years to come."

Benedict claps his hands. "We must go now," he says. "Once Nightgardin realizes Juliet is missing— if they haven't already—the Black Watch will be after her. And if they know about Damien—"

"Then there will be guns blazing by nightfall," Nikolai says. "So get your ass to the chapel and save all of our lives, Damien. For once think of someone other than yourself."

All eyes rest on me now, but I grit my teeth and stride out of the room, my shoulder brushing Nikolai's as I do.

I can physically feel his rage rising off his body like steam.

"Wait up!" Juliet says, jogging to my side. We are now some haphazard-looking entourage heading out of the palace and across the grounds to the chapel.

"What?" I ask, and this stops her short. But when I keep walking, she starts to catch up again.

"What?" she asks. "What? We're about to do something unheard of, and you don't even want to know a little about the woman with whom you are going to spend eternity."

I snort. "Eternity? This changes nothing, doll. It's a piece of paper that you can use to prove to your parents that you aren't…" The words taste bitter. "Aren't our whore. That is how you said they spoke to you, yes?"

And though she's been called the name unintentionally once by Nikolai and who knows how many times by her own parents, I'm sick at having to remind her of such a thing. I do not know this woman, but I wish her no harm. No discomfort. Perhaps this is all a game and she's playing us for fools. But to what end? It doesn't make sense—the idea of Nightgardin royalty waltzing onto palace grounds to simply use us for some deadly sport.

She falters as we make it through the chapel gates, and I instinctively grab her under the elbow. The brief touch sends an electric jolt up my forearm.

"Easy there, Princess," I say. "You need food."

She shakes her head. "I think I already proved that keeping food down isn't exactly my forte right about now. Morning sick—"

X is beside her with a clean white bag just as the wave hits, and her body convulses.

"Morning sickness," I say, finishing her sentence.

Once again, everyone stops and forms an arc around the princess. Soon to be my princess, I suppose.

"I'm fine," she insists after I roll up the bag. "But we should probably skip the whole you may now kiss the bride part?"

She grins sheepishly.

X presses a hand to an ear, then whispers something to my father.

"Go at once," the king says. "Keep whoever it is busy until we've done what's meant to be done."

X slips past us and onto the grounds.

"Everything okay, Father?" I ask, but he turns his attention to Nikolai.

"They're here."

Juliet gasps, and even I cannot feign disinterest.

"Nightgardin?" I say, teeth gritted. Because somehow I've brought this horror to Edenvale, and I don't even remember doing it.

"Hurry!" Benedict says, and he ushers us down the aisle between the pews. "Rings!" he calls out. "There must be an exchange of rings!"

"Here!" Kate calls, rushing toward us. She removes both her earrings—two silver hoops just larger than ring size, both encrusted with brilliant diamonds—and places them in Benedict's palm. "Consider it a loan until you buy her a real one."

Juliet blushes.

"Look," I finally say. "I'm doing what needs to be done for everyone involved. But let's not pretend this is going to turn into some happily-ever-after. The entire continent knows the story of what happened the last time Edenvale and Nightgardin tried to procure peace via two young lovers."

"They jumped to their deaths," Juliet says softly.

I bow dramatically, ignoring the lingering pain in my ribs.

"Exactly!" I shout, triumphant. "Maximus and Calista were fools to think they could have any sort of happiness. So please stop pretending that we will be any different."

Juliet clicks her tongue.

"What now, Princess?" I snap.

She holds her head high. "That's not how you told the story to me," she snaps. "When you took me to the Lovers' Leap, you recounted their meeting—their instantaneous love—with a wistfulness I did not think a man of your reputation capable of. And for a foolish few nights, I let myself believe that maybe we could do what they couldn't. But I realize now that the Damien I met doesn't exist anymore. Maybe he never did."

I open my mouth to deliver some sort of stinging retort, but Nikolai's phone rings. He answers and hangs it up in a matter of seconds.

"Now, Benedict," he says. "Marry them now or it's all over."

In a whirlwind of generic vows—something about sickness and health, loving and honoring—I'm suddenly sliding one of Kate's earrings onto Juliet's finger. She closes her hand into a fist to keep the dangling piece of jewelry in place.

"I do," she says with a conviction I do not understand. How could she want this—want me?

But then I hear myself saying the same words as if I'm a bystander rather than one of the main participants.

That is what I am now, what I've been for years. A bystander in my own life—never fully participating or investing. Why would I? Everyone in whom I invest, I hurt beyond repair.

I killed my mother in childbirth.

I killed my first love, Victoria.

I hear the march of footsteps beyond the chapel door and know that I've sealed Juliet's fate as well.

"I now pronounce you husband and wife," Benedict says as the doors burst open and four Nightgardin guards rush into the small church with twice as many Edenvale patrol on their heels. Benedict simply nods at our new guests.

Without thinking, I grab Juliet's hand and step off the dais.

"Stand down," I say. "All of you. By order of Damien Lorentz, Prince of Edenvale." Then I squeeze my new wife's hand.

"And by Juliet de Estel, Princess of Nightgardin and Edenvale." She rubs her hand over her stomach. "And by order of protection of the dual kingdom heir."

All guards stop in their tracks—and take a knee.

"Send word to my mother and father," Juliet says with an authoritative tone, "that I carry the first-ever Nightgardin and Edenvale heir. Send word that I will not marry the Duke of Wartson because I have wed the youngest prince of Edenvale. And send word that any other act of aggression on Nightgardin's behalf will not be tolerated."

She flashes me a questioning look, and I nod. She is Edenvale royalty now as much as she is Nightgardin.

One of the guards sneers at Juliet, and in that moment I want to rip his face clear from his skull. But then they rise and retreat.

It's all I can do to keep from applauding be- cause—well—no one's dead, yet.

"Good show," I say under my breath to my will- ing accomplice.

Juliet stands tall and regal, every bit the princess she's known to be.

"I wasn't acting," she says. "Now I think I'd like to be shown to my room. I'm exhausted."

Then she strides down the aisle and out the door.

What the hell have I just done?

Juliet

It might be my wedding day, and my first as a princess in a new realm, but I'm still alone in a high tower. I sit in front of the vanity in my chambers, brushing and plaiting my shower-damp hair when there's a knock at the door.

"Come in," I call, setting down the silver-handled brush an attendant provided upon my arrival.

Two simple words, and yet my rush of gratitude makes it almost impossible to breathe. For the past two months, no one ever bothered knocking on my door. In fact, it often seemed the Black Watch, Nightgardin's notorious secret police, took particular pleasure in barging in if I was trying to bathe or relieve myself. I was humiliated and vulnerable every waking hour.

My jaw tightens. I'll never forgive my parents for that treatment. While I know my affair could have been punishable by death, I was foolish enough to think that they needed me. After all I'm their heir, what did they gain by hurting me?

The door swings open and in rush my fellow princesses of Edenvale, Kate and Evangeline. They are each carrying a basket covered with a white linen napkin.

"Hello." My face relaxes into an uncertain smile. "Thank you for the visit."

These women are still strangers, as is this entire kingdom, so I can't help but look on every kind gesture with practiced wariness.

"We come bearing gifts," Kate chirps, setting the basket on a table and removing the covering with a flourish. "Ginger scones from the kitchen and still warm. I heard you mention you haven't been eating at the wedding and thought this might be calm enough for your digestion. Trust me, these are to die for." She pats her slim hips. "I've gone up a size since living in the palace, but Nikolai loves my new curves."

"And I brought you some art supplies." Evangeline's basket brims with adult coloring books and fine colored pencils sharpened to crisp tips.

"You came to attend to me yourselves?" I ask wonderingly. "Why not send servants to do such bidding?"

The two women exchange a short but troubled glance. "You're our sister now. When you spoke those words binding yourself to Damien, they also bound you to us," Kate says carefully. "And the child in your belly will be the cousin to any we someday carry."

Evangeline takes Kate's hand. "And trust me when I say that quick marriages run in the family," she said. "We are both more or less newlyweds ourselves. Neither of our husbands had the, ahem…patience…for a state wedding that would require years of planning."

"Nikolai compromised and promised his future coronation could receive the preparations." Kate winks, flicking her fiery red hair over one shoulder. "That kept the royal event planners from having a conniption."

I look at them, a knot forming in my throat. "But you both married men who love you, men who want you. It's plain to see that Nikolai and Benedict walk on clouds around you. When Damien looks at me it is as if I am you-know-what on the bottom of his bedroom slipper."

Kate sighs. "Neither of us had easy paths to love, but they were our journeys. You will make your own way to happiness."

"We had happiness," I choke. "Three perfect days. And then my family found me and Damien forgot everything."

"It was beaten from him, Highness."

We all turn in unison, startled at the masculine voice behind us. X straddles the windowsill.

"Where on earth did you come from?" I gasp, pressing a hand over my pounding heart.

"He always does that," Kate answers wryly. "You'll get used to it."

"I just so happened to be installing an extra security system around Princess Juliet's windows. We aren't picking up chatter that Nightgardin is planning another kidnapping attempt, but we are taking no chances with a member of our royal family."

There's that word again.

Family.

I press my hand to my lower belly. "I appreciate your efforts on my behalf."

X nods curtly. "I couldn't help overhear a few words, Highness, so please pardon my interruption. Did you know when we first found Damien that he had forgotten a year of his life? He was beaten about the head and neck as badly as a man can be and still survive. The back of his head bore bruising that was an exact match for the butt of a rifle."

I gasp, bile rising in my throat. Had Mother and

Father ordered such viciousness unleashed? It troubles me to suspect the answer.

"As the swelling in his brain has decreased, his memories have slowly returned. Like he said on your arrival, we are down to just a few lost days."

"Our days."

He nods again with a sober expression.

"Perhaps…perhaps he doesn't want to remember them." My voice breaks into a million pieces. "Pardon me, but I'm very tired. It's been a long journey and quite an eventful morning."

"I will arrange for a doctor to visit in a few days' time," Kate says before leaving. "To put your mind at ease."

"As for these—" Evangeline gestures to the coloring books "—I know they seem silly, but art has a way of healing things that seem broken."

"Thank you." And I mean every word. Their kindness is almost overwhelming. Such a rarity in my world.

The door clicks shut behind them and X moves to exit the window.

"Do you not have a harness?" I quiz, walking over. The drop is a good six stories to a flagstone courtyard.

"I used to be a free climber in the Dolomites. Don't want my skills to get rusty."

"And I don't want you to fall to the ground and crack like an egg on my account."

He tweaks one of my braids. "Then I better make you a promise that I won't fall."

A glimmer of humor ripples through me. I'd always wanted a big brother, and this man is almost the walking incarnation of the sibling I'd imagined.

"You don't need to stay cooped up in the tower," he says, swinging his feet out the window. "The grounds are extensive. There is the maze. The chapel. The wishing well. Find your new husband. Ask him to give you a tour."

I cross my arms, hugging myself close. "My new husband doesn't want anything to do with me."

"For what it's worth," X says, doing a quick, complicated maneuver that has him dangling from a near-invisible fingerhold on the castle wall, "I believe your story. That something sparked between the pair of you those missing days." He frowns. "Damien has been lost most of his life. He's weathered many storms, more than any man should for his still-short years on this earth. Perhaps you are his light in the dark."

"You care about him."

"I've always been a sucker for the underdog." A troubled look flashes over his face and disappears. "Plus I made a promise long ago to look out for him. And I don't intend to break it."

"A promise to whom?" I ask, but he is already climbing down, ducking around a carved gargoyle and leaving me with more questions than I had when I arrived.

CHAPTER SEVEN

Damien

I STORM TOWARD the open compartment of the royal hangar. After today's events—marrying a woman I don't know who's supposedly carrying my child—I need to get behind the wheel and just drive. But it looks like my brother has other plans. "What the hell do you think you're doing?"

Nikolai spins toward me with a self-satisfied grin as I watch the Alfa Romeo rise up several stories on a mechanical platform. Our great-grandfather owned a collection of rare automobiles that he kept housed here with the aircraft. The movable platforms allowed him extra storage space, but I get the feeling my dear old brother is doing more than storing my favorite car.

"You're off the racing circuit," he says, pocketing my keys. "And don't even think about trying to get it. You don't know the pass code for the lift, and I'll change it daily if I have to."

We're face-to-face now, my chest heaving. I may be his little brother, but dammit if I don't have an inch or two on him these days.

"Why?" I demand through gritted teeth. "And since when is it up to you, anyway?"

He dusts off the shoulder of my leather jacket, a condescending move that is just so…Nikolai. I know this man hates me, and I do not blame him in the least. But that doesn't mean I can't call asshole when I see it.

"Shall we count?" Nikolai asks.

"Count what?" I say, taking the bait.

He crosses his arms. "Count the times you behind a wheel has ended in some sort of catastrophe." His words hits me like a fist to the gut. "You did quite well 'rescuing' Victoria from marrying a man she only pretended to love. And now there's the lovely Juliet. Your wife. Had you not been tempting fate once again on that—that fucking death trap of a course at the Nightgardin Rally—we would not be in this precarious political position."

If I didn't know better, I'd say my brother sounded almost concerned.

"None of it has anything to do with a skull fracture or any of the other various broken bones that are still mending?" I ask, deciding to push his buttons. "That can't possibly mean a thing to you when I robbed you of your mother, your first love and now possibly your kingdom. Can it?"

My throat tightens, and the words burn like acid.

"Yes. I hold you responsible for Victoria. And for the situation we are in right now. But Mother's death? Damien, that could not be helped. Sometimes women die in childbirth, something that is beyond anyone's control." He speaks not with sympathy but with practicality. "Even Father knows that. Whatever issues you have with how you entered this world, they are yours alone. The problems caused by reckless decisions on your part? Well, those are another story."

My brother wouldn't speak to me after the accident. Wouldn't stand being in the same room with me. I was not even permitted to go to Victoria's funeral. So even though there is no affection in this conversation, it is a conversation nonetheless, the first we've truly had in years.

"I want my car, Nikolai. How the hell am I supposed to get around?"

A throat clears behind me, and I turn to see X at the hangar entrance. He's leaning on the grille of an Audi SQ5, one I never heard approach. Nor did I hear the man exit the vehicle.

"You need to stop doing that," I tell the man who has been the head of our family's security since I was a child. Back then I found his tricks amusing, always wanting to figure him out. "It's an invasion of privacy, the way you always just show up."

X straightens and brushes off his already-immaculate lapel.

"My apologies, Highness. But it goes with the territory. If you don't see me coming, neither will the enemy."

Nikolai chuckles. "Trust me. If you want anyone on your side when trouble is afoot, X is your man. Plus, now you have the answer to your question."

"My question?" As soon as the words leave my lips, I remember. "No. Uh-uh. Absofuckinglutely not. I don't need to be driven around like some pretentious prince. I go where I want, when I want."

Nikolai raises a brow. "And right now, I think you want to go where X is taking you."

He brushes past me and hops on a BMW S 1000RR. Without another word, he throws on a helmet and rides off. With my keys and the pass code to the damned car lift.

I let out a breath and make my way toward the Audi and the man who's apparently driving me to my next destination.

"I walked here," I say gruffly. "The only reason I'm letting you take me anywhere is because my ribs hurt like hell, and I'm not in the mood to walk back."

The corner of X's mouth twitches, but he doesn't exactly smile. "Of course, Your Highness."

I raise a brow. "Don't suppose you'd give me the keys to this fine-looking machine, me being your prince and all."

X opens one of the rear doors and gestures for me to get inside. "It doesn't quite work like that, Prince Damien. Besides, I think the princess would like some company."

I peek around the door to see Juliet sitting inside.

Jesus. I'm getting pretty fucking tired of surprises.

"She is your wife, Highness. It's time you get to know her."

He may be right, but for once today I'd like to do something of my choosing. I'd like to get to know her with a clear head.

I climb in beside her, and there it is—surprise number three. She doesn't even glance in my direction.

"Nice to see you, too," I mumble, staring straight ahead.

Yet despite my reluctance to be here, my shoulders relax. I am suprisingly calm in her presence, which makes me wonder if she is telling the truth about our weekend in Nightgardin.

My pinky accidentally brushes hers where it rests on the soft leather of the seat, and her hand flinches before pulling way.

She straightens, and I notice she is dressed in denim that hugs her slim curves and a pair of riding boots molded to her calves.

My cock hardens.

Casual is a good look on her.

"I can assure you, Prince Damien, that this outing was not of my choosing. If you want someone to blame for having to spend time with me, take it up with your brothers or the king."

"You're angry at me," I say.

"You left me all alone in that room up in the tower. I have no country, no home and no true ally. Your family is kind, but they are wary of me. Untrusting. I feel like the only reason they're going along with this plan is because I am now a tool that can benefit Edenvale."

I blow out a long breath. "You are not a tool to them."

She turns to me now, eyes wide. "Oh no? Then why are we here? X says that your brothers and father all seem to think a public appearance with a photo opportunity is necessary as a means to announce our marriage to the public."

"Shit," I hiss. "It'll be a glorious announcement. I can see the headline now. Two Months After Being Beaten Within an Inch of His Life, the Banished

Prince Royally Fucks Up Again. A picture of me all scarred and still bruised next to my knocked-up wife. The paper will fly off the newsstands!"

Juliet gasps, and X slams on the brakes. I growl as pain slices up my side. Apparently, we've already reached our destination. I see the royal stables outside the windshield and connect Juliet's dressed-down attire, the boots.

"Is that what you see when you look at me? The source of your royal fuckup?" She's staring at me now, her brown eyes dark and cold. "I knew that love was an illusion," she says. "I was prepared to enter into a marriage with Wartson, but when I found out I was with child, I had no choice but flee. To you. A man who seems to care only for himself."

With that she throws open her door and hops out of the vehicle, storming toward the stables.

"I wouldn't let her get on one of those horses in that state," X says, a hint of amusement in his tone. "If she's careless or spooks one of the animals, she's likely to get kicked or thrown. Then what would become of the child who could unite two kingdoms?"

I rock my head and groan.

But then I grin as an idea takes hold. I might not be able to ride fast on the open road, but I can sure as shit take off on a Thoroughbred. Right after I make sure my wife doesn't do anything so foolish.

Juliet

"I assume you have rudimentary equestrian experience?" Damien drawls as we enter the stables.

I have two choices: fight for some semblance of

inner peace or find a shovel and knock it over my new husband's smug head. "No." My one-word lie rolls off my tongue.

He scoffs. "Step aside, then. I'll ready the horses."

I oblige, not because I am helpless, but because it affords me the opportunity to watch this man who is at once so familiar and yet a stranger.

When he bends to pick up the saddle, his jeans hug his tight, muscular haunches and my breath catches.

I'm not proud, but good god, he is a perfect male specimen, hard-bodied with broad shoulders and a trim waist. His faded black denim makes love to his body, and I search out all the secret, intimate places where I've kissed, licked and bit him. I might be furious with him for forgetting me, but that doesn't change the fact that I'm drenched between my legs.

"That should do. Come on, hop up," he says, offering me a hand.

I don't need it, but I find myself taking it with a curt "thank you."

Once I'm positioned on the animal, the horse stomps once, and the pressure reverberates through my sensitive skin.

You are Juliet of Nightgardin, Protector of the Northern Ranges, Keeper of the Gardinian Legacy, Lady of the Seven Mountains and Defender of the Faith.

But these illustrious titles don't change the fact that at this moment, I'm simply a woman turned on by the father of my child, a brooding man who has forgotten my very existence.

Bitterness sours my stomach, pain eating into me like acid.

But maybe that's good. Anything is better than this unwelcome sexual craving.

"Step aside," I order Damien, seizing the reins.

"Not so fast." His arrogant brows shoot up. "You need a lesson."

My frown turns into a scowl. "I said, stand aside."

His glare could melt the polar ice caps. Why does that make him appear even sexier? I don't have time to ponder such mysteries. I must escape. Get away. Bolt to fresh air.

"Suit yourself." I tap my gelding's haunches and he responds in an instant. Damien, to his credit, assigned me to a placid beast, one who would be perfect for a beginner. My husband isn't the monster he wants to pretend. Nor does he wish to risk my neck—or the life of his unborn child.

But this animal is clearly well-schooled, and when urged knows how to run. And right now that's what I need…speed.

I'm galloping halfway down the road when Damien catches up with me. He's bareback on an Arabian.

"What the fuck are you doing?" he rages. "You told me that you couldn't ride."

"You didn't listen," I fire back. "You assumed I had limited equestrian experience."

"You answered no!"

"Because I have advanced experience, Your High-and-Mighty-Ness!" I veer off the road, click my tongue, and my horse flies over a fence with feet to spare.

"Good boy," I murmur, patting the side of his thick neck, feeling the corded muscles and pure strength. I haven't been on a horse in months. Good lord, it feels good.

From the crash behind me, it sounds like Damien isn't an amateur. He rejoins me and our horses race, stride for stride. My hair flies behind me, the ribbon tying my plait unable to withstand the wind we create.

Something rips loose within me and I let out a whoop of delight, reveling in this one heady moment of freedom, of just being a girl in the sunshine and fresh air, going faster and faster until my heart threatens to pound out of my chest.

We reach a river by an ancient stone bridge. "You deserve a drink, my friend," I croon to my horse, dismounting and leading him to drink.

"Pudding," Damien says flatly.

"Excuse me?" Is the prince hungry or has he become addled by the ride?

"The horse I gave you. His name is Pudding. Or as the groomers call him, Puddin'. He has never been considered a racehorse. If I hadn't seen you ride him with my own two eyes, I would never have believed it."

"I see. Well, it appears there is more to Puddin' than meets the eye." I tie him off to a willow tree next to the water where he can slake his thirst and enjoy nibbling the thick sweet grass.

"And you." He dismounts and draws in close. So close. And when he reaches out and lifts my chin, forcing me to stare directly into his eyes, it feels like the most natural thing in the world.

"What are you doing?" It's a wonder that I can whisper the question with my mouth this dry.

"I don't know." His voice is flint on steel. "Fuck." The desperate rasp sends a shudder along my spine. "Back in the meadow, when you were riding? You cried out, and for a moment, I swear, I remembered."

"What?" My hand trembles. "What memory did you have?"

"I don't know. It's like trying to look underwater. Everything is murky. Time feels distorted. All I know is that I was there with you, and you made a sound." He frowns. "Do I sound insane? Do you have any idea what I am talking about?"

A faint flush creeps up my cheeks. I pull my hand from his and walk to a small cluster of wildflowers, bending to pick a few. "Who can say? Apparently I have a reputation for being…noisy."

I think of the sounds I made in his arms. Whimpers. Cries. Gasps of pure pleasure.

I toss the blossoms to the grass. How I wish I could forget. My curse is that I can remember everything in perfect detail.

"My brother Nikolai used to bring me here to go fishing," Damien said after a long moment. "That is a memory that I cannot erase. He loved this bridge. It was always one of his favorite places. I hated to fish but always agreed to go."

"Why?"

He shrugs. "I idolized my brother. Both of my brothers. I'm sure they considered me a pain in the ass, but they never told me I couldn't tag along. And they looked out for me."

"You aren't close now."

"No." Darkness returns to his eyes. "I'm better

off alone. People who get close to me have a nasty habit of winding up hurt. Or worse."

I don't want to give him comfort. I don't want to risk touching him and seeing what feelings might rise to the surface for me while I'm nothing but a stranger to him. But my heart overrides my head.

"What are you doing?" he asks as I approach him, wrapping my arms around his shoulders.

"No one is better alone. Trust me. I'm something of an expert in the subject."

He is stiff, but eventually his hands find their way to my waist, and he holds me tight, burying his face in the crook of my neck.

He lets out a shuddering breath. I take one in return. And at this moment, that's enough.

CHAPTER EIGHT

Damien

SHE CRADLES MY face in her palms. Her eyes search mine, and I know what she wants to see. Recognition. But other than a moment of déjà vu, this woman is a stranger to me. A beautiful, headstrong, drive-me-crazy stranger.

She reaches up, rubs a thumb along the scar above my brow.

"Does it still hurt?" All of the earlier haughtiness disappears from her voice.

I shake my head.

She strokes a finger gingerly along my nose, and I close my eyes.

"Why does this injury seem fresher than the others?"

"It didn't heal correctly," I tell her, then blink my eyes open to meet her gaze. "After weeks of recuperation, I was rewarded with having the doctors break it again. Though I'm not quite sure I approve of their handiwork." I grab her wrist and lower her hand, but for some reason I don't let go. "Still crooked, but it's the best they could do with how badly it was injured." I paint on my devil's grin. "Now I have a whole face full of reminders of all that I've done to put my family in danger."

"You're beautiful," she blurts.

Her words are too unexpected for me shutter my reaction. My eyes go wide.

"I don't see your scars, Damien. I don't see your past. All I see is a man who has punished himself for far too long. A man who suffered great loss in his life before I even met him—and who suffers even more so because of me."

A tear streaks her cheek, and I instinctively wipe it away. Whatever happened or did not happen between us, she suffers now because of me. And I can't help think that in her eyes, I have failed her.

Just like I failed Victoria.

My father and brothers.

"Are you still angry at me?" I ask, releasing her hand.

She lets it fall against my chest. "Furious," she says, but there is no fury in her voice. "Are you not angry with me for barging into your life and messing it up even more?"

My hands rest on her hips, my fingertips kneading her soft skin beneath her riding clothes. "The angriest," I lie. Because the truth is, while I am definitely in one royal fucking mess I don't know how to clean up, right now I care nothing for the fate of Edenvale or Nightgardin. I care only that this woman has not run from me screaming. This woman I do not know who claims she carries my child.

"Juliet," I say, my mouth going dry.

"Damien," she responds.

"I—" I don't know what the hell to say, so I brush my lips against hers, testing the waters, and she whimpers, and that is answer enough.

I scoop her into my arms, and she yelps with laughter.

"What are you doing? Do you not have broken ribs that are still healing?" she scolds.

"I don't care," I growl, leaving the horses to drink while I take her to a place I have not been since I was a young teen. We weave through a copse of trees until we emerge at a circular clearing small enough that most would pass it by, but I know better.

Before fast cars, there were horses. As much as I loved my brothers, it was when I grew older that I realized I'd always live in their shadows—that there was no true place for me in the palace. So I'd ride far and fast until I found a place I could get lost.

I set Juliet on her feet, and she spins to take in the lush green canopy of the tree branches, the purple wildflowers that grow at the bases of the trunks, and a small space where a fourteen-year-old boy could hide away from the life of a prince—and where a twenty-five-year-old man can get to know the stranger who is his wife.

"Damien," she whispers. "How did you know this place was here?"

She spins to face me, a wondrous smile spread across her face.

"Let's just say I was a broody teen," I chuckle.

She brushes my hair from my forehead. "So not much has changed, then?"

I narrow my eyes, then hook a finger in the belt

loop of her body-hugging jeans. "Are you teasing me, wife?"

She skims her teeth over her bottom lip, and I wonder for a second if I've seen her do this before. I wonder how many firsts she experienced with me that I don't even remember. And it's this that makes me step away.

"We should go," I say.

Juliet squares her shoulders. "Why, Damien? Why now are you running? I am your wife. Do you still think I have ulterior motives? That I am here to be the ruin of Edenvale?"

"I don't know!" I snap, but she doesn't shrink away. She is every bit the regal princess. "I don't know you. But if you are telling the truth, then I have already failed you in so many ways. And if you are lying, then I have failed my entire kingdom. So tell me, Princess. What the hell am I supposed to do?"

She presses a palm above my heart. "What does this tell you?"

"Christ, Juliet. It's not that simple."

She doesn't falter. "I have never in my entire life believed that love was real. Only duty. My own parents would sooner hang me than show me an ounce of affection, and the one man I thought could change my mind does not remember me or trust me. Yet I'm still willing to hope. So tell me again, Damien. What does your heart tell you?"

I pull her to me, then lower her to the ground, spreading her out on her back. Her hair spreads above her like a wild crown, this princess and almost queen.

"It tells me to forget about trust and just take what I fucking want."

"Do you want me?" she asks, chest heaving.

"Yes," I grind out.

"Then take."

Juliet

He hesitates, and for a moment I think he is going to climb off and stalk away with one of his famous scowls. But then his shoulders slacken, tension releasing as he loses whatever silent battle he wages with himself. Uttering a muffled curse, he slants his full lips over my mouth. I moan as his hot tongue slides over mine in a punishing caress. He tastes like coffee and cinnamon and a flavor that is so deliciously and indescribably Damien that my heart contracts, squeezing until I'm writhing in equal parts agony and pleasure.

He presses his hips down, pinning me in place with the raw power of his erection. I've been starved of feeling, frozen like a block of ice. He burns away my defenses. I can't resist his heat.

My hands fly to his buckle as if they have a life of their own. Despite our three days of passion two months ago, I'm not an expert in the art of initiation. Instead, I fumble with the clasp, my growing determination overcoming my artlessness.

Dear God, I need to feel, to have a cathartic release.

"Juliet. No."

"What more damage can be done?" I protest. "I'm already with child."

"I don't have sex, not the way you want."

I roll my eyes, molars locked in frustration. "Hate to repeat the bad news, but you already did with me. Countless times. Multiple positions."

"I'm not denying your words." He frowns, sweat sheening his temples. "But if I can't remember being inside you, then it might as well have never happened."

"You have taken so much from me," I yell in his face, raking my nails into his neck. "Must you take even my few memories of happiness?"

One of the horses stomps in the distance, snorting a restless breath.

He blinks as if in surprise. "Juliet. I didn't mean to—"

"Forget it, Damien. Forget it…and…go fuck yourself." I choke out the profanity.

Something gleams deep in his eyes. "You're a hellcat under that prim exterior."

"Oh I've got claws." I dig deeper, and he hisses, nostrils flaring. "And if you're this committed to being miserable, then you aren't a Backdoor Baron at all…you're a Brooding Baby."

His eyes widen. "No one speaks to me this way."

"I just did."

He does something then that I never would have expected. He bursts out laughing.

This only frustrates me more. "What is so funny?"

He shrugs, a gesture so un-him. "It feels awesome to have someone bust my balls," he says. "Normally I intimidate people or piss them off."

I shoot daggers with my glare. "Well, I'm going to bust your balls with my left knee if you don't allow me to pick up what remains of my dignity and return to the stables."

"Wait one minute." He eyes me, thoughtful. "I'll let you go if that's what you truly wish. But if you do truly need…a physical release… I can help you."

My heart rate speeds up. "You'd make love to me?"

A shadow crosses his gaze. "I cannot. But I can give you pleasure. Relieve some dynamic tension."

I purse my lips. "Oh? I'm listening."

He ducks his head, inches from my face, and presses his cock right where I need it most.

I whimper. "That's not bad."

"Is that a challenge, Princess?" A wicked grin spreads across his face.

"Most assuredly." Damn the eyes of this infuriating man. I half hate him and half want him more than my next breath.

He frees his cock from his jeans and it's every inch as magnificent as I remembered. Long. Thick. Cut.

My mouth waters.

"Just as I suspected. Inside every good girl there is a bad girl waiting to come out," he drawls.

"Then free me, Prince." I roll my hips up, eager for attention. "Let's see you do your worst."

He has my pants around my ankles before I can think a coherent thought.

"These are cute." He takes in my Nightgardin-issued white cotton panties with a wolfish expression.

"Please," I plead. "I need… I need…"

"This?" He fists his cock, giving himself a slow stroke.

"You said I couldn't have that."

"Not inside," he mutters, working his fist from root to tip. "Outside? That's a whole other matter."

"Outside?"

He yanks my innocent panties to the side. "Look at your sweetness," he rasps. "Is all that honey just for me?"

Then he slides the head of his shaft over my slit. The pressure is extraordinary. He uses his length to massage my sensitive damp skin, finally centering on my bud, rubbing me in relentless circles.

I moan.

"You are a noisy one, wife of mine," he observes, eyes bright with something like approval.

"So I've been told." My toes curl. *By you*, I mentally add, before grabbing his head and hanging on as if I am drowning.

He doesn't stop or slow, and soon both of our breaths are coming fast.

He pushes his tongue into my mouth while opening my shirt, popping open the clasp to my bra.

"Jesus." He pulls back, shaking his head twice as he drinks me in. "How the hell could I forget these perfect tits?" He dips to lave one of my nipples until it pebbles and stretches taut. He is sucking me straight to heaven. Despite the sun, I swear that I see stars. The aching clench of need between my legs migrates to my chest until my entire body is primed. Even though a part of me knows that I am damned, I can't retreat from this madness. For better or worse, this man has stolen a piece of my soul.

More than any spoken vow. As if we were formed of one flesh and cleaved apart in some primal severing.

Soon I feel it. The release. It hovers before me, tantalizingly close.

He taps my clit with a clever finger, pulling back the hood and stroking the delicate bundle of nerves with all the pressure of a butterfly's wing.

I lean up and suck his neck, licking his flesh and reveling in the tangy taste. He grunts and flutters against me again and it's enough. It's more than enough.

"Damien," I moan again, unabashedly as I come as fast as an arrow shot from a quiver. "Oh God, Damien."

But even as I'm lost in this need, a new hunger builds inside me, wicked and insatiable. He has feasted on me countless times. It's my turn for a taste.

"What are you doing?" he asks as I slide down between his powerful thighs, nuzzling his steel-like erection, breathing in his hot musk.

I look up and smile at his darkly dangerous gaze. "I am going to devour you."

Then parting my lips, I do just that. My cheeks tighten, sucking him in deeper, tasting the salty skin, the burst of precum.

He pushes his hands deep into my hair, wrapping the thick strands around his fingers. I slide my tongue along his thick veins, working him gently down my throat.

I'm in many ways an innocent, and yet I know on a primal level how to do this, how to please this enigmatic man. I grip his hips and lock my gaze on this.

He seems enraged. And yet I sense it's simply

a look of ultimate concentration. He's even harder now, but I'm not stopping until every inch is mine.

"You're killing me, Princess." He thrusts between my greedy lips, fucking my hungry mouth. "How am I ever going to survive you?"

I squirm as my pussy reacts to the base need in his voice and double down on the movements. I'm artless but determined. I want to bring this powerful man to his knees with pleasure.

His balls are heavy beneath my chin and I reach out and stroke the underside.

That's enough. He goes rigid a moment before his movements grow more ragged as he spills his climax down my throat and I keep going until he's milked dry.

He closes his eyes. "When we were together before? Was it that good?"

"Better, my prince." I whisper into his ear, biting the lobe. "Even better."

CHAPTER NINE

Damien

I COLLAPSE NEXT to her, and we lie for a long while in silence—nothing but the sound of the breeze rustling the leaves. Juliet nestles her head in the crook of my shoulder, and for right now, in our hidden place, I feel like I might know what happiness feels like.

"It's beautiful," she finally says.

"What is?"

She traces lazy circles on my chest, this woman who should despise me yet somehow still wants me.

"Edenvale," she says.

I chuckle. "You've barely been beyond the palace walls."

She pushes me playfully. "I know. But it's just—different. There is a freedom here that permeates the very molecules in the air." She props herself up on one arm and looks at me. How could I forget those brown eyes? Her beautiful skin with those cheeks flushed with the afterglow of whatever the hell we just did? "I know I sound ridiculous," she continues. "But Nightgardin is different—for royalty and for commoners."

I think about Juliet's speculation that it is her own royal guard responsible for what was done to me. But then why bring me to Edenvale? Why drop me outside the hospital when they could have left me for dead, and no one would have been the wiser? I would have been another headline. Another mess for my family to clean up. If it was Nightgardin who did this to me, they must have some other motive for which I am some pawn.

"Do you really believe it was your people who almost killed me?"

Her breathing hitches. "I will never forgive myself if it is."

I skim my fingers along the line of her hair, and she turns to kiss my palm.

"Why?" I ask. "Why after all that has happened do you still want me like this?"

She kisses the scar above my eye, then the one on the side of my face. She brushes her lips gingerly over the bridge of my broken nose.

"Because I know you're still in there," she says. "I know the man I spent a magical three days with will find his way back to me."

"What man is that, Juliet?"

She smiles softly. "A man whose first instinct was to take care of me the moment you saw me. A man who let me choose and put me first." Her lips sweep across the line of my jaw. "A man who said he'd come for me when my own guards tore me away from you. And I have to believe that if you could have, you would have."

Something in me sinks. "Even before what happened to me, I never recognized myself as the guy you remember. What if he's gone for good? What if I can't ever be who you thought I was? You claim we were intimate like I've only ever been with one other person, but we both know how that ended. I am not some knight in shining armor that can save you from the evils that lurk in this world." Her expression falls, and I know I should stop. She feels something for a version of me that doesn't exist. "Juliet—I am the evil that lurks in this world. You were a fool to believe I could be anything other than what my true nature is."

I roll her off of me, pull up my jeans and stand. "We should return to the horses."

She pulls a small handkerchief from her pocket and walks to the riverbank to clean herself up. Then she rights her own clothing, transforming into a perfect princess at lightning speed.

"When will you stop punishing yourself, Damien?"

I blow out a long breath. "I'm pretty sure my life in purgatory is permanent."

I turn to leave the clearing, but she grabs my wrist with a strength and ferocity I cannot ignore.

"You do like a challenge, Damien Lorentz, Prince of Edenvale and future King of Nightgardin, do you not?"

I bark out a laugh. "I married my enemy's future queen as both our guards readied to take one or both of us down. I'd call that more of a death wish, would you not?"

"Answer me, husband. Do you or do you not love a good challenge?"

Her dark eyes burn with a fierceness that tells me

she will make a most excellent queen—if her head isn't mounted right next to mine.

"Yes," I relent. She knows that part of me well enough, at least.

She tugs at each side of my leather jacket. "I challenge you to let me show you that your heart is good and true, that you deserve more than you give yourself credit for."

I raise a brow. "And what's my end of the bargain?"

She shrugs. "Just believe that this child is yours and swear to protect it with your life. I'll prove to you and your family that my intentions for coming here are none other than to do the same. Because I know your restraint also comes from a lack of trust."

I wrap a hand around each of her wrists. "Don't take it personally, Princess. I don't trust anyone."

She rolls her eyes. "Do we have a deal, Your Highness?" Then she yanks her hands free and snakes them under my open jacket and around my waist. "Because I know exactly how we should seal it."

She is relentless, and I want nothing more than for her to be right. About all of it.

"I will protect this child," I say. "But you'll never change my mind about myself. Still, I'd sure as hell like to see you try. It'll be a good distraction from failing miserably at trying to get back those last three days."

"Or maybe it will help." She raises her brows, and I am fucking powerless against her earnestness.

I smile.

"You don't give up, do you?"

She shakes her head. Then she rises on the toes of

her riding boots and kisses me. It is not the hunger-filled need from before but something brand-new. And it's as if the very air around us shifts.

She returns to the ground, and the spell is broken.

"We should get the horses," she says. Then she laces her fingers through mine and pulls me from the clearing.

It's when she mounts Puddin' that the first flash almost blinds my vision, and the horse's front legs rise frantically in the air.

The photographer for the photo op.

"Whoa!" Juliet calls out while I still see spots of color. "Whoa, boy. That's it."

When my vision clears, she's already calmed the horse, but that doesn't stop me from stalking toward the photographer, ripping the camera from his hand and readying to smash it to pieces either on the ground or over his head.

"Damien!" Juliet cries. "Don't!" Her voice makes me pause. "This isn't the message we want to send to either of our kingdoms," she says softly. "If you do something you'll regret and word gets out…"

I look at the camera in my hand. It's a good one from what I can tell. Probably cost the guy a small fortune.

When I glance up at him, his eyes are wide with terror.

I step toward him, camera in hand, and he flinches.

"You can't surprise people like that, especially with large, unpredictable animals." He nods as I hold the camera out for him to take. "Two pictures and no flash," I add. "You almost killed my wife."

I hop onto my own horse and sidle him up next to Juliet. Her eyes are wide and her cheeks pink.

"Can we be on the record now, Your Highness?" the photographer asks.

I nod once. "Write whatever you want to write about the princess and me." I hold the reins in one hand and cradle Juliet's still-pink cheek in the other. "You like when I call you wife?" I say softly.

She grins. "I like when you want to burn the world down to protect me."

I want to tell her I'm not that guy. But instead, I turn toward the photographer and wink.

"Here's your damn photo," I say. Then I kiss my stranger-wife long and hard, feeling her skin heat beneath my palm.

If the world wants us on display, then I'm going to give it one hell of a fucking show.

Juliet

I arrive at the royal dining hall at 7:00 p.m. A note from Nikolai arrived not long after I returned from my ride with Damien requesting that I join the Lorentz family for a group meeting at that time. I want to tell them all about the new idea bursting my heart, that I establish an equine therapy program for underserved Edenvale children, but something in the brusque tone of the note has me on edge. This could be nothing but a simple family meal, but that hopefulness extinguishes as I take my seat at the long, mahogany table.

I'm the last to arrive.

The king is at the United Nations attending a diplomatic meeting, so Nikolai is seated in his place at the head of the table and staring daggers into my husband.

"Good evening, everyone," I murmur, opening my napkin and folding it over my beige sheath. Kate and Evangeline were busy in my absence, because my closet is now well-stocked with a range of elegant yet understated clothing boasting labels from Europe's top design houses. I don't have time to thank them before Nikolai snaps.

"I wouldn't say good."

Damien slams a hand on the table, the reverberation echoes to the rafters. "That's your one warning. Take your anger out on me, brother," he snarls. "Not my wife."

My brows fly up. "What's happened?" I ask my husband, my pleasure at the fact he rose to my defense overriding my concern for any misstep I've made.

"How do you think Nightgardin is going to react when they see this?" Nikolai lifts a tablet from his lap and taps something on the screen. "Ah, here it is. A Royal Mess: The Banished Prince of Edenvale Corrupts the Nightgardin Heir." He glances up, nostrils flaring. "It's from the *Rosegate Tattler*. What were you two idiots doing feeding the gossip magazines fresh fodder?"

"Wait a second," Damien says. "That wasn't someone from the Edenvale press? Juliet told me you all thought we should have a public outing—show the world that Edenvale and Nightgardin were a united front!"

He glances at me, the mistrust in his eyes all too familiar.

"I didn't lie," I say firmly.

"No," Nikolai snaps. "But I would think both of you should know the difference between a palace reporter and a Rosegate paparazzo."

I clear my throat. "We were—distracted. We didn't ask for his credentials." My cheeks flame when I think of Damien's cock between my legs, my breasts, and I squirm in my chair. "I'm sure the reports are exaggerating."

"There are pictures!" Nikolai spins the tablet around and there we are, locked in a passionate kiss atop our respective horses.

"Looks like holy matrimony suits you both," Benedict quips from across the table.

"Don't you start." Nikolai lifts a warning finger.

"Darling," Kate protests, reaching for her husband's hand.

"I'm sorry." My hackles are up. I push back my seat and stand up. "We made a mistake, yes. But we went to the stables to do what you all wanted us to do. Just because that Rosegate photographer beat yours to the punch doesn't mean my husband or I should be held at fault because the story isn't spun the way you want it. And how dare you judge, Prince Nikolai." I practically spit his name. "I lived in a veritable cloister in Nightgardin and tales of your womanizing exploits even reached my scandalized ears. You all wanted a united front, and that's exactly what we gave you, no matter what the article says."

The room falls silent.

"She has a point," Kate murmurs, her cheeks as

red as her fiery hair. "You're hardly one to wag your finger."

"Let Rosegate do their worst," Damien growls, rising to stand beside me, taking my hand. "I'll defend me and mine."

"A laudable sentiment, brother, but forgive me if I remind you that if our theories are correct, the last time you encountered the Nightgardin Black Watch, you came out worse for wear."

Damien's laugh is a harsh bark. "You almost sound worried about me."

"I was," Nikolai says quietly. His admission doesn't come easily. "You might drive me halfway to madness, but you are still my brother."

"Father sent me away, but you disowned me," Damien says, his voice tight. "Both you and Benedict did."

Nikolai rakes a hand through his hair. "The days after Victoria died, I wasn't at my best."

"It was a hard and confusing time for our family," Benedict adds quietly. "I'm not proud of my behavior and have tried to make amends."

"Hard? Confusing? That's a diplomatic way to say I murdered my brother's fiancée."

"Life is full of dark times," Evangeline finally speaks up. "Our choice lies in how we face the darkness. I've found that we can defeat the shadows only with light."

"Well said, angel." Benedict takes her hand.

Nikolai's phone rings. "Yes? Fine. Good. Right now." When he hangs up he turns to face me. "X wants to debrief you. He's picking up on Black Watch chatter. They are planning revenge for today's perceived slight."

"What will they do?" I ask in a strangled tone, hating to put anyone here in danger.

"It's Nightgardin." Nikolai shrugs. "X is hoping you can tell us."

"But… I don't know anything about the Black Watch." Does he think me a spy? Will I forever live under a cloud of mistrust and suspicion?

"You might know more than you realize," X announces, appearing through a secret door in the paneling. "There may be things you saw. Phrases you heard."

"If you're taking my wife for interrogation, then I'm coming, too," Damien says in a tone that brooks no dissent.

"I expected as much," X answers mildly. "And made the necessary preparations."

This man is an enigma. Always so calm. Would anything ever ruffle him?

"Preparations? What preparations?"

"The Eurocopter is waiting on the roof's helipad."

"Where are you taking us?" I demand as Kate summons a servant and orders a basket of rolls and cheese packed for our trip.

A small frown creeps into X's features. "I cannot say. Not here."

"But we are among family," Damien protests. "Surely you don't think Evangeline or Benedict is on the Nightgardin payroll."

"No," X says carefully. "But the walls might have ears. We don't know how the palace might have been infiltrated. We've had some—breaches recently. It might be just a precaution, but it's one I'm prepared to take. Better to think of all outcomes and be unsurprised than the alternative."

I rest a hand over my stomach. Somewhere deep inside is a tiny spark of life. A hope for a brighter future. The best parts of Damien and I merged into a new human. It seems a miracle. And one I must keep safe at all costs.

"Then let's go," I say.

"Don't forget to eat something," Kate says. "The rolls are still warm."

"Thank you," I answer. I don't add that I couldn't muster a bite with my stress. Though the smell is heavenly. That alone gives me comfort.

"Shall we, Highness?" X steps to the side with a deferential gesture.

Damien settles a hand low on my back. "After you."

His touch grounds me. It's true we have a mad desire, more chemistry than a laboratory. But is that enough?

We are both broken in our own ways. Perhaps we will end up only hurting one another, but I have to take a leap of faith.

And with that, I step through the door.

I don't know what I expected to see. Maybe a dank corridor, with moss-covered stones and the sound of distant dripping water. Instead, there is a state-of-the-art elevator. I look where the buttons should be, and there is nothing but a black screen.

"How does this thing work?" I ask.

"Fingerprint activation." X splays his big hand and a female robotic voice says, "Which floor?"

"The roof."

The doors shuts and we lurch up. Damien puts his arms around me. "Nothing bad will happen to you. I meant what I said. I will protect you."

I wish it was because he loved me, but I know it's because it's his duty.

"No matter what, swear you will protect our child." A mama bear instinct rises in me. No matter what dangers might befall us, this child must survive unharmed.

"With my life," Damien grinds out.

"Yes. Well, that got heavy fast," X murmurs as the elevator doors open onto the roof of the palace. "Let's hope it doesn't come to that."

CHAPTER TEN

Damien

I'VE RIDDEN UNBROKEN steeds and driven the fastest cars, but there is nothing to describe the feeling when X hands me the cyclic and I take control of the aircraft.

I got my pilot's license a couple years ago, but the racing circuit has given me little opportunity to fly, and I've never flown a copter such as this.

"Nikolai would not approve," I say with an air of triumph in my voice.

X quirks a brow but says nothing.

Behind me, Juliet places a hand on my shoulder, and I instinctively reach up to grab it, resting my palm over hers. A jolt of something shoots through me. Not a memory—but the memory of a feeling, like touching her is as natural as taking my next breath.

But I know this is wishful thinking, that I might feel what she feels. I refuse to believe we could have found something so real in a matter of days.

I don't do real.

I don't deserve real.

And I certainly don't trust my heart to another. I did that once, and look where I ended up.

"Have you flown before?" I ask over my shoulder.

"No," she admits. "I was never permitted to leave Nightgardin. When the king and queen were choosing my suitor, one of the requirements was for each prospect to come to court. Never was I to visit them. It would not have been appropriate for me to be seen in public."

She speaks the words like they are a script, and my blood boils to hear it—how she's been conditioned to believe she is nothing more than a means to an end. Perhaps if she were male, she'd have been raised to be a ruthless king. Instead her mother and father have stripped her of all her worth.

"I will kill them if they raise a finger in your direction," I tell her. "The king and the queen."

Her hand slips away, and she says nothing.

"May I, Your Highness?" X says, and I give him control of the craft. "It is time to land, and only I know the exact coordinates."

Below us is the smallest valley between the mountains, one I do not remember seeing on any map. As we descend, I note the smoothness of the insides of these mountains, as if they were carved by hand and not formed from generations of erosion.

"What is this place, X?" I ask.

Juliet leans forward, eyes wide, as we continue to drop down.

My ears pop, and my stomach lurches. I watch the instruments of the aircraft.

"We're below sea level, X. Where the hell are you taking us?"

X grins, a rare expression for this enigma of a man. "The safest place in the kingdom," he says.

I scoff. "The palace war room is—"

"No," X interrupts. "The palace war room is the safest place known to your people. But where we are is unknown to any. Not your father. Not Benedict. Not even Nikolai."

When we finally land, we are in what looks like a hangar save for the open sky hundreds of feet above. But then the stars disappear as something closes over us.

"Welcome," X says. "I always wondered which one of the princes would see this place first, but somewhere in the back of my mind, I knew it would be you, Prince Damien."

I shake my head, not sure what the hell this guy is talking about.

"Enough with the riddles, X. Tell me what the fuck is going on."

He turns so Juliet can see him, too.

"You're the key," he says to me. "The key to saving your family, and your kingdom."

After winding through a labyrinth of tunnels, all lined by several doors X does not take us through, we finally stop in front of one that looks no different from the rest. X pulls a key from his pocket and unlocks what looks like the entrance to a prison cell. But when we enter we find rows of desks and intricate-looking computer equipment—and a to-go coffee cup on one desk marked by a lipstick imprint. But no drinker of said coffee.

X sighs. "Always on the run," he says under his breath with a rueful sigh.

"Who?" I ask.

"What?" X counters. "Oh, I spoke aloud. Hmm... I'll have to watch that. Bad habit."

He walks up and down the rows of monitors, tapping a button here, touching a screen there. I look at Juliet, whose eyes are wide as she spins slowly to take in her surroundings. She seems as bewildered as I am—and I don't bewilder easily.

"X..." I say slowly. "Who exactly are you?"

"Damien." Juliet strides up next to me. "This man lives in the palace, knows all of its goings-on, and you don't know who he is?"

I laugh. "When you say it like that, it does sound suspect. But since I was born, X has been here. And from what I hear about the machinations of our stepmother, Adele, and a secret organization from Nightgardin trying to use Evangeline to gain access to some ancient map, Edenvale would not have escaped such peril without X's intervention. Do I know how he came to be the head of our security detail? Not entirely. But he's here, and what I do know is that we are the better for it." I say this with conviction. I may not be sure about much, but of this I am. "Still, X, old friend. You could maybe give us an answer or two. Set the princess's mind at ease?"

X spins to face us both. He straightens his tie and tugs at the cuffs of his shirt.

"It was your mother's...passing that initiated my—employment within the palace walls. But I do not work for the Edenvale government."

I shrug. "Of course not," I say. "You work private security for the royal family."

X shakes his head. "That is the part I play, yes. It is what your father and your brothers believe. But it's not the truth. At least not the whole truth."

He pulls a dagger from the cuff of his shirt.

Juliet yelps, and without thinking I pull her to me, wrapping my body around hers.

X raises his hand, and I watch him take aim—at my head.

The blade flies, and I hear it whiz past my ear. I even feel the rush of air from the speed of the steel.

But it doesn't touch me. It sinks into the wall a few feet behind me.

Juliet and I both turn to see where it landed. We approach the wall to find the point of the blade piercing the tiny body of a fly.

"Shit, X. Do you have a thing against flies?" I ask.

He stalks toward his blade, inspecting his expert throw.

"Not at all," he says. "But this is not your everyday fly. It's an escapee from our lab, which means someone forgot to seal the containment chamber. You could have been paralyzed with the juice of the Evernight poppy. It's safe enough, but what a convenient way to incapacitate an enemy. However, when the paralysis wears off—I don't think you're ready for such an experience, Princess."

Juliet lets out a nervous laugh.

"Evernight poppy? Paralysis? Flies? You speak as if you are some sort of international spy," she says.

X grins. "Now," he says, whispering so only I can hear, "we're finally getting somewhere. Juliet, if you tell me what I need to know about Nightgardin's Black Watch, I will tell your husband the truth about his mother's death."

All the blood drains from my face, and before I know what I'm doing, X's lapels are in my hand, but it takes him mere seconds to gain control, pinning me against the wall, the dagger with the poisonous insect now held inches from my throat.

"Go ahead, Princess," X says softly still. "Prove yourself to your husband and unlock the mystery of his birth."

Juliet

"I know nothing about the Black Watch. Mother doesn't permit me to sit in on her meetings with them."

"Not one?" X quizzes, a strange, tight look on his face.

I shake my head. "Never."

"Damn, I think she was right," X mutters to himself, balling his left hand in a fist and driving against his thigh. "Damn, damn, damn. I hate when that happens."

"Who?" I ask, baffled. "Who was right?"

His gaze refocuses, his eyes shuttering. "It's not time to reveal that particular part of the puzzle," he answers. "But I'm going to need both of you to take a seat."

Damien holds out a chair for me. We exchange troubled glances before I sit.

"This is bad news, isn't it?" I say to X.

He turns away, presenting me with his broad back.

What an inscrutable man. Imagine living a life so full of secrets. How does he trust anyone? And better yet, why should I trust him? But Damien and his brothers trust him—and I trust them.

"According to Section Twelve, Article Nine, Paragraph Seven of the Nightgardin Conventions of Royal Rule, the heir to the throne is to begin meeting with the Black Watch at the age of maturity, which is eighteen."

"I thought there were only eleven sections to the Conventions of Royal Rule," I remark, puzzled. "In fact, I'm certain. I had to memorize every sentence in that giant snooze fest."

X shakes his head. "There are twelve. But it appears there are people motivated in preventing you from learning all your true duties."

I gasp, as the truth slams me. "Mother? Father?"

X turns around with a short nod. "Just so."

"But…but…it doesn't make any sense. What cause would they have to hide anything from me if I'm to be Nightgardin's next queen?"

Damien's expression is one of grave realization. "Perhaps…they never intended you to rule at all." He speaks in a slow voice, a frown deepening the two lines above his crooked nose.

"But I'm their only child. The heir. The next in line. Who else is there but me? A distant third cousin? You don't understand." I speak fast. "I was raised in a strict fashion. My parents probably kept me from the Black Watch to keep me safe. To be protected from the burdens of the crown." But even as I speak, I doubt the truth to my own words. I think of the lack of affection they displayed toward me—

the threats if I ever breathed a word of my wicked weekend with Damien to anyone.

"Perhaps." X rubs the rough scruff darkening his chin. "But perhaps not. Now more than ever it's of the most vital importance for the safety of you and your unborn child to search your mind. Are there any memories that felt unsettling?"

Tears burn my eyes. "I'm not hiding anything from you. I swear on my life."

"I believe you. But to my strange secret world, of which you are glimpsing only the tip of the iceberg here tonight, it could mean a great deal. Nightgardin is the most insular country in Europe, the leadership notoriously reclusive on the world stage. It's incredibly difficult to get spies on the inside."

My eyes widen, pleading with X—with Damien—to believe me. "I won't pretend my upbringing was normal in this twenty-first-century world. I was cloistered. Not able to interact with other children once I hit puberty. I wasn't even allowed to keep a lady's maid for longer than a month. Mother said it was to keep me from doling out preferential treatment to subordinates—her words—but I think they didn't want me to form connections."

"Why?" Damien demanded. "What sadistic purpose does that serve?"

"Indeed," X murmurs. "Nightgardin is known for conservative views, but the standard to which you were kept isolated exceeds anything I've heard of."

"Wait!" Something tugs at my memories, something that only now makes me pause. "There is one thing that never made sense to me. Mother and Father had a doctor visit a couple of times a year. It wasn't the royal surgeon. It wasn't even a citizen from Nightgardin. Once I spied on their meeting and discovered that he was an American, from Los... Los Angeles. He administered injections to my parents in the face. I watched it all from a crack in the door. I didn't know what they were doing. Only that after they seemed pleased."

"Botox?" Damien asked, glancing to X.

"Or stem cells. Did it change their appearances?"

I shake my head. "Not change, but they both looked...younger after. Everyone complimented them on their seemingly eternal youth."

X jerks his head in my direction, his nostrils flaring. "What did you just say?"

I blink twice, confused. "Eternal youth."

"Yes!" X drives his fist into his thigh again. He must give himself a lot of bruises. "Yes, of course! Christ, we're finally on the right track."

And with that, he strides from the room without a backward glance.

"Track? What track?" I ask Damien once the door snicked shut.

"No clue," he mutters.

We sit in stunned silence, digesting everything we've learned since leaving the palace.

"I feel like Alice after she went through the looking glass," I whisper.

"Guess that makes me the mad hatter." Damien clears his throat. "For the record, I'm sorry about your parents. They don't seem like the sort of people who should be allowed to reproduce."

"I always thought the problem was me. That I wasn't lovable enough."

"You?" Damien's eyes widened. "That's the most absurd statement that I've ever heard."

"But is it more absurd than a secret lair in a remote mountain valley filled with state-of-the-art surveillance equipment?" I quip.

"Touché." He chuckles.

"Just so you know…I don't regret meeting you. I've lived more since our paths have crossed than I have in my entire life." I get up and kneel before his chair. He stiffens as if he wants to pull away, but I don't let him. Instead, I place my hand on his heart.

"Let me in," I whisper. "Let me find a way back to you."

He grabs my wrist. "Juliet."

The air is charged between us, thick with everything going unsaid. Then his mouth is slanting over mine, raw and hungry. Before I can return the kiss, he's moved to the sensitive hollow in my throat, sending me to heaven with his lush wet sucks.

"What do you do to me," he groans, savoring my skin in slow licks.

"The same thing you do to me." My breath is hitched but my response is assured.

"You tremble when I do this." He doesn't ask a question. So cocky. He knows he's driving me mad. "Are you tight between your legs, in that snug little pussy? Do you tremble there too?"

The door opens and I fly back, smoothing a hand over my hair, but feeling the tattle-tale blush staining my cheeks.

But it's not X who is joining us. A young woman, not much older than me with her hair in a tight bun that's as no-nonsense as her black jumpsuit, appears.

"I'm to take you somewhere more comfortable," she says in a clipped tone. Her accent is from Rose-gate.

"On whose command?" Damien asks, every inch the arrogant prince, even as I see him subtly adjust his pants due to his massive bulge.

The insides of my cheeks water. I'm so lust stricken that I barely hear her next words.

"X's, Highness. Here in The Hole, he is in charge."

"The Hole?" I inquire, trying to focus, to figure out what she is talking about.

"That's the name of our headquarters here."

"Didn't stretch any creative muscles on that one, did you?" Damien drawls.

She doesn't crack a smile. "Come. He said he'd be there shortly."

CHAPTER ELEVEN

Damien

I SPIN SLOWLY, taking in the confines of our space. I suppose it does qualify as "more comfortable" if we are comparing it to the surveillance room we just came from, but two twin beds on metal frames and a small wooden dresser hardly equate to the lap of luxury.

"We're to stay here?" Juliet asks, no attempt at masking her distaste.

"It seems so," I tell her. But the question neither of us seems to be asking is for how long.

A knock sounds on the steel door, but it opens before I can even say come in.

X enters dressed head to toe in black—black moisture-wicking shirt; black cargo pants; black hiking boots.

"Going somewhere?" I ask, brow raised.

X's stony expression doesn't change. "You two will stay here for the night."

"Why?" I demand. "I am still your prince, X. Remember that you answer to me."

It is the first time in a long while that I've thought of myself as such.

"Of course, Your Highness." X sets his shoulders, dropping his hard jaw as he meets my glare. "Though as I am not a native of Edenvale, I do not exactly answer to anyone other than my superiors."

I take a step forward, but Juliet places a calming hand on my shoulder.

"He's keeping us here to help us. I can't think of any other reason. Because if he wanted to harm us, he would have done so by now."

I take a steadying breath. "He's not going to harm us," I say. "But he is going to keep us in the dark. Aren't you, X?"

He nods curtly. "It does not help anyone to speak in what-ifs. That is my job, Highness. I find the answers needed to protect my employers."

"So that is all we've been to you for over twenty years? Your employers? Because clearly this has nothing to do with allegiance to our kingdom."

Something flashes across X's face, the first real trace of emotion I've seen since I've known the man.

"That is how it should be, Highness. It is what is best for all involved, that I do not form—attachments. But no. The Lorentz family is more than my employer. So much more than I may ever be able to reveal. But I think you know you can trust that my keeping you here is the safest option."

I grit my teeth. "I trust you," I say. "But that doesn't change the fact that I am here against my will—being kept in the dark when days of my life have already been stolen from me."

He nods. "Understood. I will brief you on what I

can in the morning. For now, take care of your wife and your child. The accommodations may be sparse, but I assure you, both of you are well taken care of."

He starts to exit.

"Wait!" Juliet says. "I do have one more question. One I hope you can answer."

X raises his brows.

"It's just—" she says. "Well, you have all this surveillance equipment. I was wondering about— the room."

A flush of heat creeps up her neck and to her cheeks, and the corner of X's mouth twitches.

"The room is private," he says. "Soundproof, too." And with that, he closes the door.

Juliet slides the door's impressive-looking dead bolt into place, then spins to face me. "I know this is all a lot to take in. I'm still reeling, myself." She steps closer. "But we're stuck here," she says, unzipping her dress. "Captive in this tiny room." She lets it fall to the floor, and all that's left is her exquisite skin, her womanly curves and a—constellation?

"Those birthmarks," I say, my voice rough as my finger traces the shape they make. An arrow.

"Yes?" she says, her voice hitching. "Damien, are you remembering something?"

I squeeze my eyes shut, willing the dark corners of my memory to come into the light. But as quickly as it came, the sense of recognition fades.

"No," I say, and I watch her expression fall. "I'm sorry."

She moves closer, stepping out of each of her shoes as she does. "About our deal in the forest by the stables," she says. "Where we apparently gave Rosegate quite the tabloid fodder."

"What about it?" I ask.

"I made some promises to you, that I'd prove my worth to your family—and your worth to yourself. But I did not ask you for anything in return."

"Except to defend our child with my life. I'd say that's a pretty tall order."

Heat floods to her cheeks. "I mean I have not asked anything of you—for me."

I cock a brow. "And now you're asking."

She nods with a shyness that makes my chest ache. "I have been a captive since the day I was born. And if what you and X think is true, it is not because the king and queen were protecting me. It is because they were controlling me. I don't want to be their puppet anymore. I don't want to be afraid." She pauses.

My hands twitch at my sides, and I know that I will explode if I do not touch her soon. But I feel like we are on the cusp of something here, and I need to hear her out.

"What do you want, Juliet?"

She skims her teeth over her bottom lip, a sexy, coy tease.

"I want you to make me your captive. And then set me free."

She unbuckles my belt and slides it free from my jeans. Then she hands it to me.

"Are you sure?" I ask her.

She nods, then heads toward one of the small beds. She reaches over her head, gripping the metal frame of the utilitarian headboard.

Neither of us says a word as I wrap the leather

around her wrists, again and again until it's tight enough to leave a mark. For a second I wonder if it hurts her, but one look at the grin on her face tells me otherwise.

I slide two fingers between her legs, and she writhes against my touch. Christ, she's drenched. This is all it takes. My cock strains against my jeans.

"Cover my eyes," she says with a whimper.

I pull my shirt over my head, rolling it up before I rest it over her eyes.

"Are you scared?" I ask.

She nods. "But I trust you, Damien. I trust you like I never should have trusted my own flesh and blood. But we are blood now. The blood of rebirth. Of new beginnings. Show me that I don't have to be scared. Show me that I'm not a prisoner anymore."

I lower my face between her thighs and give her one long slow lick from bottom to top, my tongue flicking her swollen clit.

Her arms jerk, her bound hands straining against the belt.

I plunge a finger inside her again. Then two. And then three.

She bucks against my palm, but I can still feel her restraint.

"You're no one's captive, Juliet. Least of all mine. And no one can fucking silence you anymore. So stop silencing yourself."

I pump my fingers inside her while I lap at her sensitive folds, her throbbing center.

She thrashes with wild abandon, and I can tell she is close.

"Let me hear you, Juliet."

Then I bury my face in her tangy sweetness as she lets out a fierce, guttural roar.

It is not the sound of a kept princess but that of a mighty queen.

Juliet

I am dying in the darkness, dying of undiluted, absolute pleasure. Western medical science would scoff at such a claim, but it's the truth. My truth, anyway. My body cannot contain this much bliss. But Damien isn't content with making me climax once. He won't stop. And all the while he mutters the most wicked delicious things.

"I love licking you all over."

"That's right, baby, writhe against my face. Use me as your fuck toy."

"I own this sweet pussy."

It's as if his depraved language is a key, opening something dark and wild within me.

I would slap the face of any other man who dared address me with such words. But here, tied to a bed, who knows how far under the earth, I can't get enough.

By my fourth orgasm, soundproof walls be damned, I'm sure every operative in The Hole is ready to high-five my sweet prince.

My hands fall to my sides, and I realize that I'm free. Somehow after the frenzy of my last climax, Damien unbound me without me noticing.

Grabbing me by the waist, he rolls onto his back.

"Sit on my face, Princess."

My shoulders flag. "I… I can't come again."

His green eyes gleam. "You've only just begun. In this room, in this second, I call the shots. You're mine to command."

Later I'll spend time trying to decide why words that sound so very wrong feel so very right. But for now, my body obeys his order. I slide up over his chest, until I'm hovering above his scarred yet beautiful face. I pause to admire his chiseled jaw, the arrogantly perfect bone structure, the slash of bold brows.

"Ride me hard," is all he says, before grabbing my ass and slamming me down on his hungry mouth.

My hips undulate, rocking my clit over his tongue, but this time I won't take my pleasure alone. Reaching behind, I arch my back and grab his stiff cock in my hand. The tip is slick with precum and that helps my palm glide all the way to the root. He feels amazing and I increase the speed and pressure until he's growling into my pussy.

Fair's fair. If he's my undoing, I am his. Together we might be a disaster, but we can build something beautiful with our bodies.

He jerks and I am so ready to feel his hot release, but that's not what happens. Instead, he lifts me off him and swoops me down, gliding me over the length of his cock, thrusting against me even as he doesn't penetrate. If I'd come hard before, it was nothing on these sensations. My pussy walls clench as he pumps his cock against me, driving his ass hard so that I'm bouncing. My breasts bob with the force of his sheer masculine virility.

"Fuck," he grinds out. "Jesus. Fuck. Shit."

I gasp, breath hitched, my throat so raw I couldn't make another noise, even if I wanted. Why am I not stopping, coming off this peak? Surely the ecstasy must ebb, but it's only growing.

Then he moves his fingers into the crease of my ass; I'm so wet that it's even reached there.

He presses against my hole and I can't believe what's happening. I can't believe that I am actually bucking into his touch, urging him on. When his finger is fully embedded into my backside, he takes his free hand and shoves it between my parted lips.

"Suck it," he moans, and I do, reveling in the taste of his skin.

He's filled every place that I have to be filled except the one that counts most. Then I'm on my back and he's pressing my breasts together, around his hard cock, working himself in the crease.

"Princess, I'm going to come on you. I need to mark you, do you understand? I have to do this."

I nod. For in some primal way, I do understand. Because I want to mark him, too.

I rake my nails along his spine and he comes in a thick hot spurt all over my chest. It's a royal mess, but I wouldn't have it any other way.

Afterward, we retreat to the small bathroom and slide into the steaming shower. For as depraved and ruthless as he was in the bed, now he couldn't be kinder and more gentle. He takes the bar of soap and drops to his knees, taking his time, cleaning my legs and my aching sex. Then he rises, sudsing my stomach and then my breasts. It's with some regret that I watch his semen rinse away. I feel like an addict, and Damien is my drug. I want all of him, every way he has to offer. And if he can never truly give me his heart, perhaps this overpowering physical connection will be enough.

And I'd believe the thought if not for the small, stubborn voice in my heart whispering *But will it?*

"A penny for your thoughts," he says as he massages shampoo into my scalp.

"I'd expect a prince of Edenvale to be able to afford a bit more than that," I tease.

His chuckle is low and husky. "This prince would ransom his kingdom to spend another hour with you the way we just were."

"You've been with many women," I say, hesitantly.

"Not like that."

"Your first love, Victoria. You were with her like this?" I say the words casually even as they seem to paper-cut my very soul.

"Why do you ask?" His gaze locks to mine as he rinses my hair.

"You loved her. She was your woman. You had sex with her. For Victoria you weren't some Backdoor Baron. You were Damien. I guess… I'm curious."

"You know what they say about curiosity," he mutters.

"It killed the cat?"

"I'm just saying, be careful what you wish for. You're my lawful, wedded wife. If you are in truth asking to know about Victoria, I will tell you the story. But fair warning, some things, once heard, can never be taken back."

My next breath is shaky, but my back remains unbowed. "Tell me. Tell me everything."

CHAPTER TWELVE

Damien

SINCE HER DEATH, I have spoken to no one of my affair with Victoria. Yet I cannot seem to say no to the would-be Nightgardin queen—my wife.

"When it happened," I start, "my father would hear nothing from me other than the admission that it was true—that I had not only caused the death of another, but that I had planned to steal her away from my brother."

We lie naked in one of the tiny beds, I on my back and Juliet along my side, her soft breasts pressed against my healing ribs. This way I do not have to see her expression as I reveal the worst of myself.

"Because of jealousy?" she asks, caressing the skin on my chest with the featherlight touch of her fingers.

"No," I say with mild force. "It wasn't that at all. Yes, I was envious of Nikolai. He had everything. It was all just handed to him—the looks, the charm, the women. He could have had anyone he wanted. Anyone. But when my father married Victoria's mother,

Adele, and the two came to live at the palace? He suddenly had eyes for no one other than her."

Juliet clears her throat, and her soothing touch ceases. "But—she was your stepsister."

I nod. "That was no matter. Once Adele saw that the prince—the heir, no less—had taken a liking to her daughter, it took her no time to convince Father of the match. After all, if Adele was queen, what better way to strengthen the Edenvale bloodlines but to have a second generation match as well?"

I twirl a long damp strand of Juliet's hair around my finger, but it does nothing to distract me. I know that I am here with her, in this strange place I still cannot believe exists. Yet at the same time I'm taken back six years to when I thought anything was possible. Now, of course, I know what a fool I was.

"Queen Adele," Juliet says softly. "She is the one who imprisoned Kate and tried to force your brother to marry that baroness from Rosegate."

"Yes. The family believes it wasn't just her attempt at revenge on Nikolai—whom she blames for not keeping Victoria safe. Father, my brothers and X all believe it is somehow connected to your country's attempt at infiltrating the palace."

I feel her muscles constrict at the accusation.

"I'm sorry," I tell her, and she relaxes against me. "I did not mean to—"

"Just get on with the story," she says with trepidation. "Before I lose my nerve."

"It's quite simple, really," I say. "When Victoria was betrothed to Nikolai, she was devastated. She thought him handsome, yes. And charming as fuck. But where he found himself infatuated with her, she found herself asked to play a part she did not want to play. By her own mother, of course."

I do not want to speak these final words to the fucking ceiling. So I slide to my side, stopping only when my eyes meet Juliet's.

"To this day, Nikolai will not hear me out, so promise me that if anything ever happens to me that you will tell him all of this."

She breathes in a shaky breath but nods.

"Victoria had no allies in the palace. No friends. No one she could talk to. When the betrothal was made official, she needed a place to go where she could let her true feelings be known. She wasn't coming to me. I happened to be in the garden maze when she showed up, weeping." I suck in a shuddering breath. "I didn't mean to fall for her, but it happened. For both of us. I wouldn't have tried to run if she hadn't asked. I wouldn't have turned from my brother like that if I didn't think that the first time I fell in love would be the only time. Christ, Juliet. I was a kid—a teenager. I thought I had all the answers and that as long as she and I loved each other, we were invincible. Haven't you ever done something so fucking stupid all in the name of love?"

I don't wait for her to answer. I squeeze my eyes shut, trying to lock away the memory of Victoria looking to me for solace—to make everything better.

But I don't see my first love in my mind's eyes. Instead, I see a broken shoe. An injured knee.

"Damien?" Juliet sounds worried, but I can't open my eyes. I won't—not until the vision becomes clear. Because this vision feels more like a memory.

"Damien!" she says again, this time with more

force. "What's wrong? Does something hurt? Oh God, did—did I break something when I—"

The vision fades, and I'm forced back to the here and now.

I open my eyes to find hers wide with worry. She searches my still-bruised face—runs soft fingers over my healing ribs, and I grab her wrist.

"I'm okay," I say, and I feel a weight lift. Or maybe something in the air shifts.

"Then what was that?" she asks. "What the hell happened?"

"I loved her," I say plainly, and I can see Juliet try to shutter an emotion, but fear is hard to hide. "But it's not her I see behind closed lids. Not anymore."

She worries her bottom lip between her teeth.

I return to my memory, the one that hovers elusive and out of reach. "Did you...on the night we met... were you—injured?"

She sucks in a breath, and a tear streaks down her cheek.

"The heel of my shoe broke, and I'd fallen and skinned my knee. My stupid palms, too. I swear I was like a toddler playing dress-up that night, and I—" She gasps again. "Damien...how did you know that?"

I grin—not because I think I've found closure with at least my own feelings about my first love, even though I'm pretty sure I finally have.

I grin and kiss my wife, because when I closed my eyes, I saw her.

It's nothing more than a snippet of the time that was stolen from me, but it's something. It means I'm getting close.

"I believe you," I say. "I can't remember anything

more than a broken shoe and your injured leg, but I believe you."

She forces a smile, and I understand.

I remember a sliver of that first night. But I don't remember her like she wants me to. I don't remember what I felt that possessed me to make love to her like I'd only ever done with my own brother's intended. I don't remember falling in love.

But maybe I don't need to. Maybe letting go of Victoria means I can fall all over again.

For now there are no right words, so she lets me kiss her until both our eyes fall heavy. And for the first night since I've been home, I sleep without waking from dreams or guilt—my beautiful, patient, pregnant wife's limbs entwined with mine.

Juliet

We wake to a knock at the door.

"Are you two decent?" It's X.

I fly to my feet, grabbing my scattered clothes in a pell-mell motion before dressing as if in a race. Damien doesn't stir. It seems cruel to wake him when he is so peaceful. Even as I'm struggling into my bra, I take the time to study his face. The way his full lips part in slumber. The impossibly long length of his lashes.

Despite the tattoos and scars, I don't see a bad boy. I see a lost man. Someone who has been starved of love and affection and cursed, hated and feared. A man who never complained, never cracked, who made himself as hard as granite to face an even harder world.

And as ridiculous as it seems, given the strength of all those cut muscles, one thought rises above all others.

"I will protect you," I whisper.

He's been hurt so many times. I won't hurt him again.

I crack open the door. X is alone. He is polite enough not to swing his eyes in the direction of the bed. I wonder if he knows what happened in here. If the power of our passion tattooed the very air.

"Can we talk?" he asks in a quiet voice.

"Alone? I don't want to wake the prince."

"I'd prefer you didn't." His enigmatic eyes give nothing away. Not for the first time I wonder, Who is this man?

With regret I slide from the sanctuary of our sparse yet somehow perfect bedroom, quietly closing the door.

As we head down the hall, X gives me a sidelong glance. "I understand you were quite…passionate last night."

I dig in my heels, refusing to take another step. "You said there were no cameras."

"There were not. And the room is soundproofed. Or so we had assumed. Either I need to write a sternly worded letter to the door company or you two are more powerful than some of the most state-of-the-art security equipment."

A blush creeps up my cheeks.

"No one minds around here," X answers. "I think in truth, everyone was a little jealous."

"Why?"

"We aren't a monastic order. Nor do we prize virginity. But working in The Hole takes single-minded commitment and mission focus. This means that when our operatives are stationed here they agree to celibacy for the duration. Keeps things simple. So I'm sure many were biting their knuckles last night."

He chuckles, something that seems so not X. But then again, he is a man of mystery. Everything about him surprises me.

"You're—celibate?" I blurt, not able to believe a man so virile would deny himself physical release.

"Me?" That earns an honest peal of laughter. "I'm not assigned to The Hole. I've been in the field for years…which allows me to play the field."

"But there isn't anyone special?"

His unexpected mirth fades. "In my line of work, it is strongly discouraged to get close to anyone. It's not safe, for others or for us."

"Can you be reassigned to The Hole?"

He shrugs. "Sure. If I piss off the right person. Luckily I have a very influential friend who makes sure I don't."

"Who's that?"

He presses his hand against a screen, and sliding doors open.

"Just wait."

I enter a meeting room empty but for a massive table surrounded by twelve chairs.

"What's happening?" I ask.

"Hello, Juliet," a woman purrs in my ear.

I turn, startled, swearing no one had been there a moment before. Now an attractive middle-aged woman sizes me up with intelligent eyes. Eyes that are a brilliant, stunning green. Eyes that I've only ever seen on the faces of the three princes of Edenvale.

"It's a pleasure to meet you at last," the woman says, moving to a seat at the head of the table. She wears black knee-high boots; the stiletto heels are at least five inches and thin as toothpicks.

She exudes power, arrogance and brains.

I feel like a naive schoolgirl in comparison.

"Who are you?" I ask.

"That's an interesting question," she says, crossing her legs. "X, bring our guest a mug of Belgian hot chocolate, light on the whipped cream. That's the way you like it, yes?"

X bows once and is on his way.

"How did you know my favorite drink?"

"Another interesting question." The woman trails a finger over her lower lip. I don't know what she's hoping to learn from my features, but it's as if she's memorizing every detail. "I propose a trade. Every time you answer three of my questions, I answer one of yours."

"But that's not fair."

"No," she says, sighing. "But life's not fair, is it?"

I narrow my gaze. If she does indeed know who I am, then she should treat me with the reverence fit for a future queen. "Very well. What do you want to know?"

"Did you want to rule Nightgardin?"

The way she pronounces the name of my kingdom, it's with a native-born tongue. She's one of my subjects, if I could call her that. I get the sense she answers to nobody and no one.

"I did," I respond. "But not as my parents

intended—kept by a man for whom I cared nothing and who himself cared no more for me than as a means to an end."

She leans closer. "Did you ever get the sense that your life was in danger? Were you exposed to any strange accidents? Especially in the past five years?"

"Accidents?" I frown. "There was a fire at our summer estate. And once when I was riding my horse on a mountain trail a large boulder was dislodged from above."

She steeples her fingers. "Did you ever wonder if these…accidents were intentional?"

"Not until now," I say curtly. "That's three questions. Here's mine. Who are you?"

"No one."

"That's not an answer," I scoff.

She arches a brow. "It's the truth. I am a woman without a country. Without a name. Without a claim to anything or anyone."

"Why?"

She bites the corner of her lower lip. "That's another question. You owe me three. Did your parents ever mention anything to you about a spring?"

My brows furrow. "Spring? Like in the woods? Or something mechanical?"

She doesn't crack a smile.

"Why would they mention springs to me?" Nothing this woman says makes any sense. "They didn't speak to me unless it was to remind me to know my place. To stay out of sight. To not bring undue attention to myself."

"And you never wondered why they insisted on keeping you from your subjects?"

"That was the custom."

"It never used to be." The woman's smile is cold.

"What are you trying to say?" I fly to my feet, voice shaking. "My parents weren't the best. They didn't show me love in the usual way. But they aren't murderers. They weren't plotting to burn me to death or crush me with a boulder."

There's the sound of a scuffle outside. I hear X's voice.

"I'm sorry, but you can't go in there."

"Like hell you'll keep me from her," Damien snarls. "Juliet. Juliet!" I can hear his panic and imagine how he must have felt waking up alone. Not knowing if I was taken.

"So dramatic, that one," the woman says with something approaching affection.

"Damien!" I call out. "I'm in here. I'm safe."

The doors open and he rushes in. "Thank God. I had a dream—no, a fucking nightmare." He pulls me to him, presses his lips to my forehead. "But you're safe."

"I am. But not if you listen to her." I jerk my thumb to the head of the table, but when we both turn around, the woman is gone.

CHAPTER THIRTEEN

Damien

"SLOW DOWN," I tell Juliet, who's speaking so fast I can't tell if she's upset or excited.

"This woman, she said she had no name or country or anything. She said my parents were plotting to kill me. And she kept talking about some spring, wanting to know if I knew anything about it."

I stumble backward and collapse into a chair. "Jesus," I hiss under my breath.

Juliet rushes to me. "What is it?" she asks. "Does something hurt?"

For a second I chuckle. "Everything hurts, Princess. After what we did in that room last night, I wouldn't be surprised if the ribs re-broke." I pinch the bridge of my nose, feeling the slight bump that means it will always be crooked, that I will never quite be the me I was before I was sent away.

She lowers to her knee, resting her palms on my thigh. "I'm sorry," she says. "I—"

"Don't you ever apologize for what you do to me, Juliet. I am a fucking animal when it comes to you, and I would have it no other way."

She smiles coyly. "Okay. But, then, what's eating you? Did I upset you?"

"You mentioned a spring—or that this strange woman mentioned it."

"It's true," X says from the doorway. "My associate needs to know what Nightgardin knows of the spring. Because the more they believe the lore, the more they will want to breach every barrier we—I mean Edenvale has."

Juliet straightens and throws her hands in the air.

"Will someone please tell me what the hell is with this damned spring?"

My eyes and X's widen.

"Your Highness," X says, sauntering into the room like he's done this a hundred times. He probably has. "Several months ago Princess Evangeline was taken captive and dragged into the palace's catacombs."

Juliet falls into one of the chairs now, too.

"This is all too much," she says breathlessly. "First Damien gets me pregnant. Then he forgets who I am. Rosegate tricks us and turns an amazing morning outside the stables into tabloid fodder. And now there are catacombs and a mystery woman—even more mysterious than X—who knows how I take my hot chocolate, is asking me about springs I've never heard of, and who can disappear into thin air the second I turn around."

X clears his throat.

"It's just one spring, Princess."

She glares at him. "Then tell me what is so special about the one spring."

I blow out a long breath. "Benedict's wife—Princess

Evangeline—she almost died to protect it. But I don't know a hell of a lot more than that."

X takes a seat across from me, and Juliet and I both stare at him expectantly.

"It is what The Order here in this part of the continent has been sworn to protect—the Spring of Youth."

I laugh, but X's countenance does not change. "You're serious. About a magical spring and some order who protects it? And you are a member of The Order?"

Yes. Growing up as a royal is a life less ordinary. But I never anticipated spies, murder plots and a magical goddamn spring.

He rolls up his sleeve, revealing the tattoo of a crow's feather on his forearm. "You think me a spy, and perhaps that is one way to look at what I do. I go places others wouldn't dare to go. I obtain information others would never be able to find. But first and foremost, I protect that which needs protecting."

"The royal family," Juliet interrupts.

X nods once. "For centuries Nightgardin and Edenvale have been at odds over one thing."

I roll my eyes. "Yes," I say impatiently. "Power. We have it, and Nightgardin wants it."

"You have power, yes." X raises his brows. "But it is access to the Edenvale catacombs they want."

"Oh my God," Juliet says, realization creeping into her tone. "They think they can rule forever." Her jaw tightens, and angry tears brim over her lashes. "If this spring is real and it does what they think it can do?" Her hand flies to her mouth. "The fire. The boulder. And—and—there must have been other times they tried and failed. I was never meant to be queen, was I?" Her eyes are wild. "Tell me, X! That woman asked about accidents, but I don't think it was because she didn't know my answers. She was testing me—testing my loyalty to my family. But you already know, don't you? You've known this whole time!"

X slides his chair backward, but Juliet shakes her head.

"Don't move. Don't come near me. Just. Tell me. The truth," she says, holding out a hand to ward him off.

X freezes in place. "You were to be murdered on your wedding night, the Duke of Wartson framed, and your parents left without an heir."

She chokes out a sob. "Why does it even matter to them whether I live or die? The throne is not mine until they're dead and gone."

X shakes his head slowly. "There have been whispers in the Order of your father's concern over your mother's behavior, of his threat to abdicate, which would strip your mother of her power and give the throne to you. But with you gone he will not risk it, not without an heir of his choosing."

She swipes at the tears streaming down her cheeks. "Father has never spoken of this to me. He's never given any indication that he even cares for me let alone wants me to rule."

"You knew, Juliet," he continues. "Somehow you knew the marriage wasn't right, so you fled."

She stares at me now, and she is not the timid girl I thought she was. She is a woman betrayed, scorned, by everyone she thought cared for her. Not just her parents, but me.

"I went looking for pleasure. I went looking to have one joyful experience that was just for me."

"And Prince Damien saved your life," X says carefully.

She pushes her own chair back and stands abruptly, pointing at me. "He—he doesn't even know me! My mother wants me dead, and my own husband doesn't remember falling for me! I have no one," she says. "If not for my unborn child, I am completely alone. And they will not take my baby from me."

She starts toward the door.

"Juliet—" I stand and take a step to her, but what comes next? What do I say to right all the wrong that has been done to her?

"You can't fix this," she says, tears streaking her cheeks.

I venture another step, trying not to spook her, though I know in this place she can't go far. So far she doesn't run.

"You're half right," I tell her when we are face-to-face. "I don't remember." Her dark eyes—full of so much anger and hurt—bore into mine. "But you aren't alone." I cradle her face in my palms. "You and this baby. Let me protect you both." I kiss her, and I feel some of the tension leave her body. But she's still holding something back. "Let me fall for you both and prove myself worthy of a love as big as yours."

She melts into me then, and I don't care that X is still here. I kiss her hard, my lips on hers a promise. One I hope I can keep.

Juliet

At last X clears his throat.

"As much as I hate standing in the way of true love, we need to get to the palace."

"This isn't true love," I hasten to say, pulling back, Damien's unique minty flavor lingering on my tongue. I swear he's permeated every cell of my body from the way I tingle.

"That a fact?" X says in a sardonic voice.

"It's animal magnetism. And pregnancy hormones." I refuse to meet my husband's eyes. I hope my lie sounds believable to his ears. I hate to have him pity me. He's said he wants to fall for me, but that means he's not yet fallen, and maybe he never will. But he wants me—wants to pleasure me and protect me—and I tell myself if that's all we ever are, it's enough.

It has to be.

Without another look, I march forward down the corridor until I come to a halt at a T-junction. "I don't know which way to go," I admit, turning around.

Damien and X watch me, each with something simmering in their eyes. X is full of his usual secrets, and Damien? Who knows how many levels my brooding prince has, but he's retreated far into himself.

For a moment I wonder if I wounded him with my quick denial of how I feel, but I know that's impossible. Just as much as I know my own desperate, pathetic truth.

The truth strikes me with lightning precision, igniting my core.

I'm in love with my husband.

Desperately.

Irrevocably.

Always and forever.

"We turn left here, Highness," X says with a gentle gesture.

I hate that I feel he can hear my thoughts.

As I pass by he adds, "I know you two won't want to be late."

"For what?" Damien growls, stalking beside me, looking neither left nor right.

There are so many doors along this hall. None marked. The Hole is as mysterious as The Order. As X himself.

"Your first sonogram." X stops in front of a door that looks exactly the same as the three on either side. He presses his hand to a keypad, and it opens up into an elevator. The same in which we arrived.

By the time we step outside, blinking at the sun, the chopper purring on the helipad, my heart is in my throat.

We are going to see the baby. Our baby.

"Are you excited?" I ask Damien as we strap into our jump seats and buckle matching Kevlar helmets under our chins. X and my husband sit up in the front while I take a position near the window.

"Yeah. Sure." He smiles over his shoulder in my direction, but the grin doesn't reach his eyes.

My heart sinks faster than a pebble tossed into the deep end of the ocean. No matter what he said before, in The Hole, his actions speak louder. The helicopter lurches into the air, drops as we hit a patch of turbulence. I grip my seat, terrified, alone.

Then Damien reaches his hand back to take mine, knowing that I need it without even turning around.

I lace my fingers with his and squeeze once. He does the same in return.

Beneath us the mountains drop into tight, twisty valleys, a geographical maze, much like the paradox holding on to me as if he'll never let go.

He can claim me with such passion and then retreat into a part of himself that I don't think I'll ever be able to breach. The walls are too high.

But as I rest my free hand on my stomach, tears sheen my eyes. Damien is more than I could have hoped for, even if he cannot give me every part of himself. "Remember, you never believed in happy endings," I whisper.

"What was that, Princess?" X asks, eagle-eared as always.

"I was wondering how much longer," I say with feigned enthusiasm. "I'm ever so eager for the sonogram."

"Twenty more minutes the way I fly." X pulls hard, giving more throttle.

True to his word, we land on the palace roof exactly twenty minutes later. Two nurses are waiting for us.

"Right this way, Prince Damien, Princess Juliet," one says while the other simply gawks as if we are some kind of celebrities.

Damien's jaw is tight.

If my stomach has sunk to the bottom of the ocean, it's now burrowing deep into the sand.

"Are you not looking forward to seeing your child?" I say in a light tone. "Because you're welcome to go to your quarters and refresh yourself. It's been a long night and——"

"What?" He grabs me by the elbow, swinging me to him. "What are you saying? This is my child. Our child."

"You haven't seemed interested in taking part since X mentioned it earlier."

His face softens, even as his eyes remain vacant and haunted. "It's not the child. It's going to the hospital. I haven't been there since my discharge and…" His Adam's apple bobs heavily. "It's not a place that I'm eager to see again so soon."

"I see," I say softly, resting my hand on his cheek. And I do. Suddenly all his actions are clear. What a self-absorbed drama queen I've been. Damien isn't upset to see the baby. He is worried about returning to a place where he suffered, where he woke without memories, without hope.

"See this?" This time I take his hand in mine. "This time it's my turn to hold your hand. And Damien?" I rise up on my tiptoes and press my lips to his ear. "I'm never going to let you go."

"Thank you," he says in a husky whisper. "You're more than I deserve."

We leave the roof and make our way down to a waiting Rolls-Royce. The royal hospital is a short drive away and we are greeted by a team of attending doctors, in addition to the two nurses who accompanied us.

"This seems like overkill," I murmur to him.

"It's Edenvale," he says, shrugging. "They love their royal family."

My throat tightens as I think of the contrast to my

own kingdom. To my parents, who would have been willing to kill me to keep claim on the throne for an unnatural tenure. But with effort, I push the dark thoughts away, because there is no room for gloom at this moment. We are to see our child.

"Ready?" Damien asks me.

"Ready," I say, and we step out into the sun.

CHAPTER FOURTEEN

Damien

JULIET GRIPS MY hand tightly as we emerge from the Rolls. Only it's not just a team of doctors waiting for us.

There are cameras.

The bright morning sun is the least of our worries as state-of-the-art flashbulbs blink and blind us.

"Prince Damien! Was it a royal plot to knock up the Nightgardin princess?"

"Your Highness! Where will you and the princess reside?"

"Princess Juliet—is it true Damien doesn't even remember sleeping with you? How can we be so sure you're carrying Edenvale's heir?"

"Damien, are you even welcome in Nightgardin now that you've made a whore of the princess?"

At this Juliet gasps, then stumbles over a paparazzo's shoe. But before she hits the pavement, I scoop her into my arms. She ducks her head into my chest.

"Enough!" I bark at the crowd. "No fucking comment!"

I storm for the doors where X ushers the medical team and us inside.

"My apologies, Highness," he says once we are safe from the press. "I assure you that no one knew of this appointment other than myself and the medical staff."

I lower Juliet to the ground, and though she stands fine on her own two feet, she is shaking. "Someone leaked it," I growl. "And this isn't like the Rosegate stunt at the stables. That was international press out there, descending like damned vultures."

X nods. "Your Highness," he says to Juliet, "I will get to the bottom of this and assure it will not happen to you again."

"Thank you," she says, an audible tremble in her voice.

As the team leads us to a private elevator and then up to the birthing ward, I make myself clear to each and every one of them.

"When we find out who made our presence known, there will be consequences. Juliet is Edenvale royalty now, and whichever one of you betrayed your very own princess will have to deal with me personally."

I stop suddenly as the elevator doors open onto our floor.

"What is it?" Juliet asks, giving my hand a reassuring squeeze.

Your very own princess.

I shake my head. "Nothing," I tell her, but it's a lie. Yet the truth doesn't make sense—that I've spoken those very words before in my wife's defense. Because if that is the case, it means I've not only forgotten making love to her, but I've also forgotten failing her once already.

"I'll do a paternity test," Juliet says softly as we head toward the exam room. "If you're still having doubts about—you know."

It's not a matter of whether or not I want the test. Ever since DNA testing became possible, Edenvale used the medical advancement as another form of protection against enemies like Nightgardin. Ultimately, I have to break the news that it will be required by royal law to determine if she is, in fact, carrying an Edenvale heir. But royal law is not what is important to me right now. Nor do I want to risk hurting her.

"It's my baby," I say, jaw tight. "You have nothing to prove to me, Princess." Then I wrap my arm around her, and we walk side by side into the room.

"X," I say before I close the door and he stands guard. "What happened downstairs is one thing," I say. "But if anything else gets leaked—we're talking about the safety of our baby."

"Of course, Your Highness. From here on out it will just be the doctor and the two of you," he says, and the reassurance of his tone is enough for me to believe that for now, we are safe.

The obstetrician, Dr. Dominique Broussard, guides Juliet to the exam chair where a gown sits folded. "Please put that on," she says in a kind voice. "The opening should be in the front. I'll return in a few minutes, and we'll get started on all the fun."

The doctor steps out of the room, and for a few long seconds, Juliet and I stand there.

"Can I help you out of your dress?" I finally say.

She blushes, but I know it is not the same kind of reaction as when she disrobed for me last night.

"You can grab the zipper if you want."

She turns so her back is to me, pulling her long brown hair off her neck.

Unable to resist, I press my lips to her nape and breathe her in. Then I watch as goose bumps pepper her flesh, grinning in silent satisfaction at how this woman reacts to my touch.

"Damien," she warns as I slide the zipper down and push the dress off her shoulders.

I chuckle but say nothing as she steps out of the dress and then into the exam gown before situating herself on the chair.

A knock sounds on the door. Perfect timing.

"We're ready," Juliet calls out, and Dr. Broussard reenters the room.

"Is this your first doctor's visit, Princess?" she asks as she situates herself on the rolling chair parked by a counter full of equipment. "I mean—for the baby?"

Juliet nods nervously. "I fled my country before getting medical verification of the pregnancy. But I—I stole a test from the bath chamber of the servants' quarters. I needed to be sure before I risked running away." Her cheeks redden. "I thought charting my fertility was foolproof, but I guess our baby had other plans." Her hand instinctively flies to her belly. "I'm just realizing now how scared I am. I mean, what if the baby's not okay? What if the stress of running from home had some sort of adverse effect? What if—"

I grab her free hand and hold it tight. I will not

discount her worries. They are valid, and I won't lie that I don't share some of them as well. But she doesn't have to worry alone.

"Whatever we find out today, we find out together," I tell her, and her brown eyes shine as she nods.

"The best thing you can do, Princess, is to relax. The calmer you are, the easier it will be to find the baby on the sonogram. But please do not get scared if we don't. You're barely ten weeks. Sometimes the baby is so small that we cannot find it on the first try."

Juliet sucks in a shaky breath, then blows it out slowly.

"That's good," the doctor says. "Deep, calming breaths."

As Juliet inhales and exhales, so do I.

"We're going to make you a bit more comfortable," Dr. Broussard says, and presses a button that tilts the chair so that Juliet is reclined.

All the while, her hand remains in mine.

Dr. Broussard opens Juliet's gown. "Don't worry, this won't hurt, and we're nice enough to heat the gel for you."

She squirts the small tube onto Juliet's belly, then swirls it around with some sort of wand, her eyes trained on a monitor to her right.

It's so quiet in this sterile room. Too quiet. In my head I hear the steady beep of the heart monitor in the hospital room where I woke up only a couple months ago—practically at the same time this life was conceived. But I remind myself that this is not the same thing. No one's life hangs in the balance, least of all my own.

"Hmm..." Dr. Broussard says, and Juliet sucks in a breath.

This brings me back to the moment, and I realize I'm holding mine. Because hmm, in my opinion, isn't what we want to hear.

The doctor's brow furrows as she presses the wand firmly to Juliet's abdomen, swiping it slowly from left to right. "Ah!" She finally relaxes. "I think that inhale of yours shifted us right into the perfect position, because look." She points at what seems to be a small smudge on the black-and-white screen. But then I notice that the smudge has a pulse.

"Damien," Juliet whispers. Her voice catches on the last syllable of my name. "Can you see it?"

I squint at first, not ready to believe my eyes. But it is no trick of the light or glitch on the screen.

I clear my throat and squeeze her hand, but I cannot find the right words. Nothing has ever hit me so hard, not since losing Victoria. But this is no loss. It is the greatest gift given to someone who has never deserved so much. I do not need a fucking paternity test to tell me what I already know. Because there, on the screen, is our baby's beating heart.

Juliet

"Do you?" I ask Damien again. "Do you see our sweet little gummy bear?"

"Gummy bear?" He groans, but I can see the smile tugging at his lips. "That right there is the most gorgeous child that has ever existed on the face of this planet. Tell me, Doctor, have you ever seen a more perfect baby?"

Dr. Broussard chuckles. "It is indeed one fine-looking fetus, Highness. You're measuring about nine weeks, which puts the date of conception—"

"Right after the Nightgardin Rally," I say, coyly glancing to Damien.

Molten lava has nothing on the intensity of his answering gaze.

The little gummy bear on the screen flutters about as if reacting to my increased pulse rate. "It's incredible that it can move so much and yet I can't feel it."

"Well, right now it's not much bigger than a grape. It will take time before it makes its presence known, but don't worry. Soon it will be waking you up from a sound sleep with a sturdy kick."

I burst out laughing. "I'm really going to have a baby."

"Yes." Damien kisses me on the forehead. "We are."

"Would you like some photographs?" Dr. Broussard asks.

"As many as you can give us," Damien orders, his face still buried in my hair, breathing me in as if I am his only source of air.

"Wonderful. Let me finish taking a few more measurements and then you two can get to the Prenatal Genetic Center for the lab work."

I stiffen at the term *genetic*, studying the doctor's face, but she doesn't seem overly concerned, just a busy professional who must see a hundred couples like us every week.

"You are sure everything you saw today was

okay?" I ask, trying to force a smile. "Not to be a nervous first-time mother but…I'm a nervous first-time mother."

She nods. "This is still early days for a pregnancy, but I can assure you that everything that I've seen so far is perfectly normal."

"So why the blood work and genetic lab?" I ask.

"Ah, that's for the paternity test. Standard procedure given the circumstances."

"I see." But I don't. Damien says he believes me that the child is his, and yet here we are, walking to a lab as if we are a couple on one of those American reality shows trying to prove who my baby daddy is.

It's dreadful.

"You don't have to do this," Damien says once we are alone in yet another hospital room. "I don't care about royal law. If I say it's my child, it's my child."

I shake my head. "If I don't, you will always wonder," I say flatly. "So will the kingdom. And your brothers."

"Juliet—"

There is a knock on the door and yet another doctor breezes in. This one carries a tray covered by a blue surgical cloth.

"Good morning," she says, holding the door open with her foot. "Right this way, Prince Damien. The waiting room is to the left."

"Waiting room?" Damien snaps. "I'm waiting right here while you draw my wife's blood."

"Sorry, official hospital policy. Only the patient and the doctor can be in a room together during a paternity draw. Prevents tampering."

My husband growls, a feral, animalistic warning from deep in his throat. "I'm not going one step."

"Just listen to the doctor." I sigh. "Let's get this over with."

"But I should be here, with you."

I shrug. "And right now I would rather be alone. Just go drink some coffee and I'll be out before you know it." My head is swimming as I try to process the fact that I'm really doing this, that I'm going to have a baby. Being here in the hospital makes it all so real. Every once in a while it's as if the insanity that is my current life bears down like a pile of bricks. It's hard to stand strong and carry all the feelings.

"You'd do well to listen," the doctor says with a tight smile. "Happy wife, happy life."

He kisses my cheek, his lips lingering for a moment, and I can hear a note of unease in his shaky breath. "Fine," he says. And when he straightens I see that same unease in his eyes. I've hurt him by dismissing him. But I just want all of this over with.

For a moment I want to call him, but my attention is drawn to the doctor. The woman is in her fifties with a silver bob and pair of blue glasses. She seems perfectly ordinary, so why are my senses on high alert?

"Onto the table," she says, fiddling with her instrument case. "Please expose your belly. I'm assuming you want to get out of here and back to your comfortable palace, so—" She nods toward the exam table.

I do as she says even as I wonder why she wants to draw my blood from there and not my arm.

The doctor approaches me with a syringe not for

drawing fluids but for injecting me. Before I have a chance to react, she jabs the needle into my skin, pressing the plunger and filling my veins with a yellow liquid. I take three sharp breaths. It burns. I want to ask why. I want to fight. But my vision blurs. I should scream. Or panic. But I can barely move.

Or breathe.

The doctor touches her ear. "The deed is done," she mutters, not in a lilting Edenvale dialect but a thick Nightgardin accent, and before my world spins black I realize the horrible truth.

She is Black Watch.

What a naive fool I was to think I could ever be safe. My hands rise to my belly with the last of my strength.

The door bursts open, and two figures barge into the room, but I can barely make out their shapes. My vision grows darker with each labored breath. I can't move.

"Here!" a male voice calls—familiar, yet I cannot place it. "Damn, they've given her the milk from the Evernight poppy. How the hell did they even come across it? Very few know of its potent qualities, which means if Nightgardin does, they're a more powerful enemy than even I anticipated." The man swears. "Get that antidote to her lips. There isn't a second to lose."

"On it."

Damien?

One of the figures tips something against my frozen lips. A bitter taste floods my senses like I've taken a shot of dandelion root juice. What about the Gummy Bear? Will it be okay?

"That should counter the paralyzing aspects in a few minutes," the other voice calls, and I swear it is X.

There is the sound of a scuffle, and I hear someone grunt.

"Fair warning, Princess, as I know you can hear me," X continues, his features taking shape as my vision begins to clear. "The child will be fine. The Evernight poppy cannot harm it, neither can the antidote, which will soon allow you movement. However, I must let you know that the Evernight poppy comes with a host of rather exciting side effects."

I flex my hands and sit up. "Are you sure the baby will be okay?"

He flings out his arm, grabbing the Black Watch operative by the neck, and the woman goes limp as a rag doll. "Don't worry, Princess," he says to me as I gape in horror. "I just knocked her out cold. She won't be feeling anything for a while—unlike you."

The moment he says the words an intense clench of need bears down between my thighs. My pussy is suddenly aflame with a hunger like I've never known.

"You must get her home without a second to spare," X orders to Damien. "This one has to come to The Hole with me so The Order can begin the interrogation. If they gave her the poppy that meant they wanted Juliet alive…and I'm going to find out why."

"Then make her wish she was never born," Damien snarls.

"You focus on your lane. Trust me. Your hands are about to get very full. But don't worry, one orgasm will be enough to counteract the poison's effects… It is potent enough."

If he says anything else it's drowned out by my own moan. The Black Watch operative nearly poisoned me, but whatever exciting side effect X referred to feels almost as deadly.

My back bows as my hips undulate. If I don't have physical release soon I will die.

CHAPTER FIFTEEN

Damien

I CARRY JULIET to a staff-only elevator. She writhes in my arms.

"What is happening to me?" she cries.

"It must be the aftereffect of the drug you were given," I say through gritted teeth.

I stepped away from her before when something in my gut told me I shouldn't. I put her in harm's way. If X hadn't found the real genetics doctor bleeding from a head wound on the landing of a stairwell, where would Juliet be now? What would the Black Watch be doing to her?

"How did they get to me?" Juliet asks, and then she moans in my arms.

I let out a bitter laugh. "They breached the one place we couldn't stay away from with you in your condition—the hospital. They've been unable to infiltrate the palace, but we didn't anticipate this."

"Damien," she cries, then spins in my arms, hooking her legs around my hips. "Damien, you have to make it stop!"

I can't think straight, so I hit the emergency button on the elevator, and we jerk to a halt.

"Make what stop?" I ask.

Her eyes plead with mine.

"I need to come." She squeezes her knees around my hips and slides up and down against me.

My cock hardens, my body betraying my animalistic desires.

"I have to have you inside me," she grinds out. "Fill me up and give me release, or I swear to you this ache will kill me!"

She hops down and tears at the button of my jeans, then yanks my zipper open.

"Now," she gasps. "Take me now!"

She hikes up her dress, revealing no panties underneath.

Christ.

She grips my thick shaft with her fist and rubs my slick tip up and down her folds.

I growl. *"Juliet,"* I grind out, and she whimpers.

"Inside me!" she wails, but I will not take her like this. Even in her state, I will not lose control. Because I have failed her like I failed Victoria. Just as I knew I would. But I will give her pleasure. I will give her release. She deserves love and protection, but I am good for only one thing.

"Turn around," I tell her.

Her breath hitches, and she stills. "But I thought—" she starts, a sobering look in her eyes. "I thought after last night…after seeing our baby… Damien, I know you don't remember us, but I also know that you feel something."

"All I feel, Princess, is the truth. I destroy everything that is good and pure. Know that my family will protect you and this child, but I will return to my life of banishment—for their safety and yours."

She turns, her back to me now, and she presses against my erection.

"Do what you're good at, then," she snaps with bitter resignation. "Give me what I need and then do what you do best. Leave."

She reaches behind me and grabs my shaking palm and pulls it around her hips and between her legs. My finger brushes her wet, swollen clit, and she whimpers, her beautiful, innocent ass rubbing against my cock.

"Do it!" she orders, and I plunge one finger inside her, then two, and then three.

She bucks as I pump in and out, as I drag my soaked fingers up and down her heated folds.

She is an animal, riding my palm like no woman has done before, and I silently curse X for not truly preparing me for what was happening to her.

My tip presses against her ass. I could enter her like this. She would let me past that final threshold.

But it would be a line crossed over which I could never go back. Taking her like this would mean she was no different than any other woman I'd been with since Victoria. And I would have to live with the knowledge of hurting her like that.

I slide my fingers from inside her and swirl them around her clit. She cries out, reaching a hand behind me and grabbing my shaft.

"Do it, Damien! Fucking do it!" Juliet yells. But that is not the voice of my Juliet. That is not the mother of my child, the woman I love.

Because I do love her, dammit, even if I am poison.

I bring her to climax with my hand alone, and when she's done bucking and thrashing—when she falls limp against me—I catch her as her knees go weak. Only when she steadies do I let go, pulling up my pants over my now-painful erection.

"Damien," she says, voice shaky.

"Are you okay?" I ask, my voice hoarse against the knot in my throat.

She nods.

"You deserve better," I tell her. It is the truth—the only truth I can tell her. "Now we must get you and the baby to safety."

I start the elevator again, and we both ride to the main level in silence.

Only when we reach the bottom does Juliet break the silence. "I know what you're thinking," she says. "And it's not your fault."

My jaw tightens. "You don't get it. I ruin everyone and everything. I can't do this."

Her eyes grow wide. "What are you saying?"

I clear my throat. "I'm saying that you will be cared for and protected by my family. But you will be a princess without a prince. It is not as if I've been officially reinstated. It will be best for everyone if the banishment sticks. I am sorry, Juliet."

The doors open, and there before us are a host of guards, but they are no guards of Edenvale.

"Good morning, Princess," one jeers, and I swear I've heard that voice before. "We've been waiting for you."

Juliet opens her mouth to scream, but one of the

Black Watch yanks her from the elevator car and clamps a hand over her lips.

"Get her to the car," the first guard sneers. "And be careful. She's a biter."

He shakes out his hand, and I note the scars on both the back and his palm. Whatever happened before Juliet came to find me, this bastard had his hands on her—and she made him bleed for it.

She kicks and flails, and something in me breaks. I launch myself at the man who holds her, my fist connecting with his face. I feel bone crunch.

A fist jabs into my side—into my still-healing ribs—and I crumple to the floor, gasping for breath.

The first guard stands above me, grinning.

"Are we going to do our dance again, young Prince?" He glances over his shoulder to where Juliet stands captive. "Let her watch this time. Let her see what awaits her in the public square tonight."

I roar through the pain and try to climb to my feet, but the man of the Watch pulls a handgun from his side and swings it at my head. Right before everything goes black, I hear Juliet scream.

Juliet

In my life, I have known soul-crushing boredom. I have drunk deep from the well of loneliness. I have felt passion grip me in its jaws and tear me to a place between agony and ecstasy. And I have known the awe-inspiring, almost holy sensation of being in love and getting that love returned.

But I've never known hatred—true hatred—until this moment. Bile burns my throat as I fight like a cornered lioness surrounded by jackals. I'm fighting for more than my own life. This is about my unborn child and Damien cold-cocked and discarded on the cold elevator floor like yesterday's trash.

One of the abductors carrying me turns my body toward his chest as he adjusts to my thrashing weight. The acrid scent of his body odor assaults my senses. He reeks like liverwurst and stale aquavit. I don't hesitate, lunging forward and sinking my teeth through his shirt until I connect with the hard muscle beneath.

Unlike Damien's powerful body, which exudes a need to protect, this man gives off an air of cruelty and small-mindedness. He wants to hurt me, so I hurt him first and make it count.

He bellows as my teeth clamp down, and I twist my head back and forth to deepen his pain. I don't know what has come over me, only that the whole world has turned hazy and red.

I channel my inner bulldog, driven by a primal need to defend my child. In the background, I am dimly aware of pain in my skull as the man yanks fistfuls of my hair in an attempt to stop my assault.

My eyes burn, watering from the agony. I can hear strands of my hair giving way as roots are pried from the scalp. But I don't stop biting because maybe I am buying myself and my baby a few more precious seconds of time. Even now members of The Order might be assembling to come to our aid. And with any luck they will find Damien. Fear creeps into my heart with a reptilian coolness. The last time the Black Watch got their evil hands on him he lost so much. Can he withstand a second assault?

The world explodes in a white light. A dull, heavy sound of metal striking bone reverberates to my core. My body goes limp as a warm, sticky liquid slides down my neck. As I'm shoved into the cramped darkness of a trunk, a man stares at me with a leering smile, a steel club clutched in one beefy hand.

"Time to go home, Your Highness," he chortles before slamming the lid.

I part my lips to scream but can only muster a weak mewl before I lose consciousness completely.

I don't know how long I remain in the trunk. Every so often I start to wake, unable to see anything, not even my hand before my face. Holding my stomach, I croon snippets of lullabies from my country. Not songs my mother ever sang to me, but those my nursemaids and nannies used to comfort me as a child. The lyrics are pretty and silly about mountains and snow, little trolls and wildflowers.

"It's a beautiful place," I whisper before my world goes dark yet again. This is how I spend the ride to my home country—in the trunk of a car, falling in and out of consciousness.

Yes, Nightgardin is a proud, timeless land forged from ancient glaciers and wild rivers. Its people are good and hardworking even if the ruling class is corrupted to the core. If I find a way to survive the trials ahead, I will figure out how to reforge the monarchy into an institution that can make my people proud once again. Where young women are respected and advanced just like any son.

But first I need to live long enough to defeat my parents.

The trunk opens a few hours later and I push myself to sitting, dehydrated with a splitting headache and my hair matted with my own blood.

I look around, realizing where my abductors have brought me—the Nightgardin Stables. Once it was a place of refuge and freedom for me, but today it may well become my doom.

"Darling," a woman croons in the shadow, stepping forward to take the shape of my mother. She looks like a Renaissance painting of a Madonna with her long thick hair and lovely features. The trouble comes when you get a good look at her eyes, which are devoid of any human compassion or love.

"What have you done, Mother?" I growl as if a fierce voice can cover the fact that my legs are so weak they can barely support me. A pitchfork leans against the closest stable, the home of my favorite stallion, Loratio. If I grab it I could... I could...

"You wouldn't murder your own mother, now would you?" she asks with a soft smile, her gaze following mine to the tool.

"No." My voice is choked. "I'm not like you."

"That's right." She watches me with her flat, dead eyes. "You're not."

Then she snaps her fingers, and the Black Watch goons reappear.

"Tie her up!" she orders. "And put her in the empty stall beside Loratio."

"What are you going to do to me?"

"Me?" My mother adjusts her long gray dress and transforms her face to the picture of grief. "I'm not going to do anything. The Black Watch, however, will show the public what happens to those who com-

mit treason. Because isn't that what you've done...
darling?"

"You're insane," I whisper.

She smiles sweetly, though there is no trace of
anything sweet in this woman's body. "Not at all,
darling. I am a woman who knows what she loves,
and in my case it's power. I thought we could tame
you—that we could stomp out that spark we saw
from the beginning. But when you ran off, we knew
you were beyond our control."

"So you decided to murder me and pin it on Wartson."

She raises a brow. "Look at you, Juliet. You've
learned so much in your absence. Have you not? You
might have actually made a good queen were I ever
willing to give up the throne."

She laughs, but it is without an ounce of true
mirth.

"You can't eliminate me," I say. "The Black Watch
abducted me right in front of Damien. He saw everything even as your filthy servants beat him—just
like I know they did last time. Soon everyone will
know their queen is not a queen of the people but a
ruthless, heartless witch who cares only for herself."

I have to believe—even after what he almost did
in that elevator—that Damien will come for me. I
know what it meant for him to have wanted to take
me from behind, that I am no different from the
countless others who have come after Victoria. But
I also know that he is as invested in this child as I
am. If it is not me he loves and wishes to save, he
will come for his heir.

She simply shrugs as her minions seize my arms.

"What does it matter when he's the one who ruined Nightgardin's future queen? In this country, my subjects will only care about one version of the truth… mine. The rest is fake news."

"Where is Father?" I cry out as the men drag me to the stable. Of my two parents, he's always been the kinder one. That's not saying a lot, but I can't imagine he would be in favor of murdering his only child in a bid to rule forever—not when they could lock me away in a tower and never let me see the outside world again. It is a fate unimaginable, but at least my baby would live.

"Detained," she says as if confirming my thoughts. "My consort is in the palace gaol deciding whether he is with me, the true daughter of Nightgardin, or against me."

She turns and begins to walk away.

"If there even is a spring, you will never get to it. The Lorentz family has protection the likes of which you will never know!" I cry. "You won't win, no matter what you do. Even if you kill me and your grandchild."

She spins to me, a viper ready to strike. "You think The Order can protect them? We've eliminated their members before, and we will do it again." She saunters toward me with such ire in her eyes, the likes of which I've never seen. The strike across the face comes before I have time to anticipate it. I cry out and then taste blood. "Gag her," my mother says to a member of the Watch without glancing back. "Let my daughter spend her last few hours on this earth in silent contemplation of her many sins."

CHAPTER SIXTEEN

Damien

THE FLOOR BENEATH me jerks, and I get the sensation of falling. My stomach roils, and my head throbs against the cold, hard ground on which I lay.

Snatches of images play against the screen of my closed lids like a strange kaleidoscope.

Dressing a wound on Juliet's knee.

Juliet riding next to me in the Alfa Romeo, my hand between her legs.

Juliet naked and beautiful and trusting in the hotel penthouse, my hands on her, my fingers in her.

Juliet assuring me that she isn't fertile, that it is safe for me to be inside her like this.

My eyes open wide, and I scramble to my knees only to fall forward, so dizzy my stomach threatens to empty itself right here on the floor. But I fight the nausea, fight the searing pain in my head. Then I grip the metal bar that runs the perimeter of the cage I'm in—the hospital elevator—and I pull myself to standing just as I stop moving and the door slides open.

"Jesus, Damien. What the fucking hell have you done now?"

My brother Nikolai and his wife, Princess Kate, stare at me, mouths agape.

Then Kate swats him on the shoulder. "He's hurt, Nikolai. Help him."

I reach a hand for the spot on my temple where that bastard nailed me with his gun. I feel the drying blood even as more trickles from the still-open wound.

"Juliet," I say, my mouth dry and voice hoarse. "They took Juliet. Someone needs to get to her now." I take a step forward across the threshold of the elevator doors. Then I stumble. Nikolai grabs my shoulders, righting me before I hit the ground.

"Nightgardin?" he asks, and I nod.

"He needs stitches," Kate says. "We need to get him to the ER. I don't think there's anything they can do—"

"No," Nikolai says. "If they didn't kill him, it's because they meant for him to be found once again. If anyone from the Black Watch is still here, they'll expect him to end up in emergency care. We can patch him up in the prenatal ward as well as anywhere else."

Something registers that didn't before. The sound of babies crying—a nearby nursery.

I look from Kate to Nikolai, from Nikolai to Kate. The reason for their visit to the hospital now snaps into place.

"It appears congratulations are in order," I say, and Kate's cheeks flush. "You're pregnant?"

"Eight weeks along. It seems there will be cousins growing up together in the palace," Nikolai says with a grin, and I realize it is the first he's smiled in my presence since my return.

I open my mouth to respond, but Nikolai cuts me off.

"Someone is coming," he says. "Can you walk?"

I nod, though it may be a lie.

"I'll distract whoever it is," Kate says. "Just get him to safety."

"Juliet," I say again, then splay my hand on the wall to find purchase as dizziness strikes again.

"She's safe," Nikolai says. "At least until nightfall."

He doesn't explain further, just leads me to a small hallway and then to a door. He grips the handle only to find it is locked, but this doesn't deter him. He grabs a small, sharp tool from his pocket and expertly slides it into the lock, the door clicking open as he does.

Then we are inside a storage room. But this is no room full of cleaning supplies and rolls of bathroom tissue.

"Surgical supplies?" I ask as my brother flips on a light.

"You can't leave like this," he says, his eyes full of concern. "It's a bad gash. If you keep bleeding you might lose consciousness behind the wheel, and—"

I clear my throat as he swipes items from the shelves. Hydrogen peroxide. Iodine. Gauze. A surgical needle and thread.

"I know you think I was drinking. That you need some bigger answer as to why I left with Victoria that night," I say. "But you know the truth. You know she did not leave with me against her will. And you know that I never would have put her in harm's way. If I'd known that storm was coming—that the streets would be so slick..."

His jaw tightens as he readies the materials. "She's dead, Damien," he says. "Don't you think it was bad enough she wanted you instead of me? It doesn't change the fact that I loved her and lost her twice in the span of one night. But I will not let you die for it."

He puts on a pair of latex gloves and cleans the wound over my eye, but he won't look directly at me. So I grab the collar of his shirt and force him to.

"I loved her, too, Nikolai. I loved her and lost her and wasn't even allowed to fucking mourn her. At least you got that. And now you have Kate. And a baby on the way. I'm sorry for what I did, but I can't change it. I can't take it back. I get it," I say. "I'm poison to anyone I love. I can't seem to escape that. But you can at least acknowledge that I lost something, too."

He raises a syringe. "This is gonna hurt."

Then he stabs my skin with the needle, and I hiss through clenched teeth. But by the time he depresses the plunger, I can already feel the cool prickle of the numbing agent kicking in.

"And here I thought you'd sew me up without anesthetic," I say. "Where the hell did you learn this little trick, anyway?"

The corner of his mouth twitches. "Spend enough time with X, brother, and you'll learn a thing or two."

"He teach you lock-picking, too?" I ask as he begins to suture the wound.

Nikolai shakes his head. "Learned that when I

was thirteen and wanted to get into the wine cellar for a little taste."

I wince as the needle hits a piece of skin that isn't quite numb.

"Sorry," he says, and I actually think he means it. "But we need to get you patched up and out of here."

"How do you know Juliet is safe?" I ask.

My brother's jaw twitches, a subtle nervous tell. "X called and told me what happened after Juliet's sonogram. He wanted to make sure Kate and I were safe since he knew we were here as well. He mentioned something about a live broadcast Nightgardin had prepared for this evening but assumed it had nothing to do with Juliet since she was safe."

"But she's not," I growl.

Nikolai shakes his head.

"Three times I failed her," I say. "Twice today—and the first time when they took her from me in Nightgardin."

Nikolai's eyes widen. "You remember?"

He ties off another suture, and I nod. "It's my baby," I say. "I have no doubt."

"You love her," he says with realization.

"Since the moment I laid eyes on her after the Nightgardin Rally. Though now, after what happened before they took her, she must think…"

"Done," Nikolai says. "Eleven sutures. You lost a lot of blood, but the dizziness will hopefully subside soon." He pulls something from his pocket and places it in my palm.

The key to the Alfa Romeo.

"I might have taken it for a little spin this morning," he says with a wink. "It's parked out back. Kate and I will call for a car to get home."

"What makes you think I won't fail again?" I ask.

Nikolai shakes his head. "It's time I admit that I failed Victoria, too. I knew she was unhappy but refused to believe she could want anything other than what she was being offered—the chance to be queen. The monarchy is important, but it took me a long time to learn that other things rank as high."

I chuckle. "Are you about to lecture me on the merits of true love?"

He removes the surgical gloves and crosses his arms.

"You're the one living out the legend of Maximus and Calista," he said. "Go rescue your queen, but please avoid the whole Lovers' Leap part of the story."

I grip the key in my palm. "I'll never get past the Nightgardin gates in a fucking race car," I say. "They'll hear me a mile away."

Nikolai's phone buzzes, and he pulls it from his jacket pocket. He laughs softly as he reads the text, then turns the screen to face me. It's a text from X.

Please inform Prince Damien that alternate transportation awaits him at the Rosegate and Nightgardin border. Good luck and Godspeed.

"How the hell did he—?"

"You know better than to question the inimitable skills of a man called X," Nikolai interrupts.

"Thank you, brother," I tell him, and then I'm out

the door, racing for the stairwell because fuck if I'll step into an elevator again.

And then I'm behind the wheel—a place that used to spell death and destruction, or at least my wish for them. I start the engine with renewed purpose, then glance in the mirror to check my brother's handiwork.

I am beaten, bloodied and scarred—marked with reminders of the mistakes I've made.

But I am no longer broken without repair, not if Juliet still believes in me. I just have to get to her in time.

Good thing I know how to drive fast.

Juliet

A brown mouse furtively runs along the stable wall in the direction of the burlap feed bag in the corner. Normally the sight would fill me with fear, send me screaming in the opposite direction. But now I can't even muster the energy to watch it climb up to feast inside the oats. It turns out there are far worse fears to face in this world than a marshmallow-sized rodent.

And tonight I shall be subjected to them all.

Nightgardin has never signed on to any international treaty banning torture. Despite decades of intense lobbying from human rights groups, the monarchy has steadfastly maintained the position that no outside body will ever regulate the kingdom's operations. We are ruled by direct reign, although I had privately planned to make changes when I took the throne, to ensure our small country looked forward and embraced change.

But I never had a chance. My mother plans to rule forever.

A furious tear slides down my cheek, echoing the trickle of blood coursing down each forearm as I tear the flesh from my wrists. I won't be able to instill any progressive changes. I can't even free myself from these stupid ropes pinning my hands above my head.

There's a tightening in my abdomen, a spasm of contracting muscles. It can't be the baby stirring as it's still far too small, but it's a persistent sensation.

A flicker.

A flame.

As much as I want to give up hope and try to prepare for the horror to come, I can't ignore the little warmth.

It's love. Love for Damien. Love for the child we created in three nights of passion. Love for the potential we hold if only there is a way.

Even in all this darkness, love—a fantasy I never believed to be real—still exists.

I suck a shuddering gulp of air deep into my lungs and set my jaw. I have no idea how I will survive this night, but I have to try to believe. Even if the Black Watch does take my life in a few short hours, it can't take the power of this love from me.

And that has to count for something.

A heavy march of combat boots on flagstones draws closer. They halt outside the stable.

Boom! Boom! Boom! comes the bang of a drum, the execution drum.

Four Black Watch soldiers enter my stable, their

faces obscured by black ski masks. I've heard stories of Nightgardin public executions. They aren't common, saved only for those who commit the worst offenses against the state. There were a few in my childhood, but I was never allowed to watch. At the time, I thought my parents were trying to protect my innocence. Now I realize that they simply didn't want me in public. I was the princess intended to be kept out of sight and out of mind.

I wince when one of the guards removes a sharp blade from a scabbard, but they won't hurt me away from the lights and cameras. Instead, he cuts my bonds and my arms collapse against my sides like two sacks of potatoes.

"She put up quite a fight earlier," one tells the man beside him. "Sent Captain Augustin to the hospital to get stitches."

I can't restrain a smile at that news.

"We could muzzle her," one growls.

The biggest one steps forward and cracks his knuckles. "Or knock her teeth out."

"Enough." A fifth man enters the stable. He's got a puckered empty hole where his left eye should be and a large angry scar that distorts half of his face. "You have your orders. The princess is to be left unharmed until the broadcast begins."

Ah yes. There is a twisted ritual to my death. Protocols must be preserved.

The man with the missing eye reaches out to grab my arm, and I spit in his face.

I won't make this easy.

But he throws me over his shoulder as if I weigh nothing and begins striding away. Loratio, my stallion, stomps and huffs as I pass, but to no avail. I beat on the man's back and shoulders, but I might as well be caressing him for as much as it seems to bother him.

Minutes later, we come to a stop beneath a platform draped in purple velvet and bearing the Nightgardin crest. Upon it are two high-backed chairs, one occupied and one empty. My mother is dressed head to toe in white, her face somber, her hair tied in a severe knot. She looks as pure and merciless as the Old Testament God.

She rises and steps forward. "Good people of Nightgardin, it is with a heavy heart that we gather here on this evening to bear witness to what happens to those who betray the kingdom. No one is above the law, from the farmer in the fields to our very own princess in the palace. A crime against the state is a crime against us all, and the penalty for treason is…death. Princess Juliet, as the Queen of Nightgardin, I condemn you to one hundred lashes for your crimes. After which your body will be burned, living or dead, in an attempt at purification. May God have mercy on your soul."

The drum beats three times, and she takes her seat on a high throne. My father isn't there. He must not have yielded. Perhaps he will burn tomorrow night.

The crowd is utterly silent. I feel the heat of thousands of eyes on my body. The quiet will not last long. I won't be able to endure one hundred lashes, let alone fire, in silence. But I will not give my mother the show she desires.

"A word, Mother," I call out, and the crowd stirs. They aren't expecting this. No one talks back to the queen in our kingdom. "You might burn my body tonight, but there is a flame that you'll never be able to extinguish, that of the love that I bear for my husband, Damien, Prince of Edenvale, and our unborn child whose life you will snuff out as well. Some fires burn too bright. May God have mercy on your soul for trying to stop true love."

The uneasy murmurs in the crowd increase. Even the guards on either side of me seem uncertain what to do next.

Finally, Mother rises again. "Proceed," she says in a tight, high voice. This isn't going according to her plans. She expected me to meet my fate like a sacrificial lamb. Instead, I've shown her a boldness she never knew was there—a boldness I never knew I possessed until I met Damien Lorentz, banished prince of our sworn enemy, Edenvale.

I've been the good, obedient daughter for too long, and look where it got me. Now it's time for me to be a strong woman who doesn't go down without a fight.

"I said, proceed," Mother says again, her voice rising, going hard and ugly. "Make it two hundred lashes, and anyone who hesitates can join her."

That jolts the guards out of their stupor, and they begin dragging me toward the stake.

"This is murder!" I scream. "You are killing your own child—your own grandchild—for the crime of love when you know that's not your true motivation. The only reason you are taking my life is for your own ambition. You are the guilty one."

My words are brave, but my strength is no match for these men. They bind me to the stake, but no one meets my eyes. The drum beats louder and louder, playing my death song.

I lift my eyes to the sky in time to see a shooting star cut across the horizon. And here at the end of it all, without hope, but full of love, I whisper my final wish.

CHAPTER SEVENTEEN

Damien

AS INSTRUCTED, I park the Alfa Romeo in a wooded area a few miles outside the Nightgardin border. Air travel would have been too noticeable, yet I fear none of that matters now. Even though I made it here faster than anyone should be able to drive, it still took hours—excruciating hours where I had to be alone with my own thoughts, imagining what that ruthless witch and her spineless king might be doing to Juliet.

Juliet, who thinks I forgot her.

Juliet, who thinks I cannot love her.

Juliet, who may not be alive by the time I get to her.

As soon as I exit the vehicle, something rustles in the brush up ahead.

I've been in a bar brawl or ten. I can hold my own if my hands are not bound behind my back or if I'm not clocked upside the head with a fucking pistol. But I didn't think of obtaining a weapon before I hopped in my car and drove—my singular focus getting to my wife and child in time to save them both. I hadn't really thought about the how.

The sound comes again; this time the entire bush shakes.

"Show yourself," I say, readying myself for hand-to-hand combat.

A horse whinnies and my shoulders drop. I follow the sound, guided only by the light of the moon. On the other side of the tree is a white steed roped to a branch. A quiver of arrows and a bow are strapped to his saddle, and I outright laugh. Because this is X's doing.

Who the hell is that guy?

Pinned to the quiver is a note as well.

Your Highness,

This is Maximus. He will obey your every command as he has been trained by The Order to be ridden by you and only you.

"How?" I ask aloud, then continue to read.

Do not ask how. You should know better than that by now. All you need to know is that you can trust this horse to get you to Juliet, and he, in turn, will trust you. Do not leave his side, and you will be safe.

I shake my head and chuckle, yet I know to heed X's words. He saved Nikolai and Kate from our overambitious stepmother. He stopped Rosegate from using Benedict's wife Evangeline to gain access to the map that leads to the spring—if it even exists.

With a bow, arrows and a hell of a lot of hope, I untie the horse, mount it and kick my heels against his flanks.

"Yah, Maximus!" I call, and we take off into the night.

* * *

My years of exile have taken me all over the world, but I always felt a strong pull toward Nightgardin, despite its differences with Edenvale. Perhaps on some level I was drawn to Juliet. Whatever the reason may be, it is why I've spent the bulk of my banishment years right here in these lands, which means I know them almost as well as I know the land of my birth.

We traverse the woods on the east side of the royal grounds because it is the only place where we can hide in the cover of dark. The royal square rests in the center of the gated lands. So all we have to do is make it past the east gate guards, and we're in.

Easier said than done.

Even if I can aim and shoot an arrow, I do not wish to strike first. Plus, they will all be armed with guns.

Maximus rears his head, impatient.

"Not yet," I whisper, inching him closer to the forest's edge. "Not yet."

Then an idea takes hold.

I pat the pocket of my jacket and grin when I find what I hoped would be there—a lighter.

Nightgardin cigars are illegal in Edenvale, but hell if they aren't the best. I don't partake often, but when I do, I like to be prepared.

I tear off my jacket and then my shirt. I wrap the latter around the shaft of an arrow, near the tip.

"On my count, Maximus," I say, praying that X's words are true, that I can trust this steed.

I tie off the shirt, making sure it won't give way. Then I set it ablaze.

"Three...two...one. Now, Maximus!"

He rears on his hind legs and sprints from the

cover of trees. As soon as we come into the well-lit perimeter of the palace gates, I find what I knew would be there—the electrical transformer that powers most—if not all—the property that lies beyond the gates.

As Maximus gallops toward the gates at top speed, I ready my bow, aim and shoot.

Sparks fly, and the wooden pole on which the transformer rests catches fire. Guards run both toward it and away from it in mass confusion, and I notice that these are not the Black Watch.

I grit my teeth. The Watch, in its entirety, is in the square doing who knows what to my wife. My child.

My horse and I are steadfast in our purpose—making it to the gate.

A gate that is far too tall for him to clear. But he doesn't slow, nor do I command him to do so because this is our only chance. Either we die on this side or die trying to get over it.

As shouts of "Trespasser!" and "Shoot!" ring out among the chaos, Maximus reaches the gate—and we fly.

Or at least it feels like we do.

Shots ring out, and I hiss as white-hot pain slices through the skin on my shoulder just as Maximus's back legs clear the only thing barring me from my wife.

As we slam into the ground, I give myself a split second to check my wound.

Blood runs along my bare arm, and I remember that my shirt is at the burning end of an arrow—my jacket most likely on the forest floor. I have no protection other than speed and my archer's aim.

But it's nothing more than a graze. It's nothing I won't endure to save those I love.

My wife. Our child. The fates of our two kingdoms.

Stay alive, Juliet. I will find you.

Juliet

The chief executioner kneels. "For what I am about to do, Highness, I am gravely sorry and humbly beg for your forgiveness."

I stare at the man who will bring about my end. In my country, it is custom for the condemned prisoner to absolve the guard assigned to take their life. Everything has a ritual here, even state-sanctioned murder.

"No." My voice is clear and strong. "If you do this you shall kill your future queen and the heir to come after me. I offer no forgiveness for such an act."

A ripple passes through the crowd. My reaction is unanticipated. I'm not playing their game by their rules any longer. Because I won't stand silent as I'm tortured and my unborn child dies in my body for my mother's insane ambition.

The murmurs in the crowd grow louder and I see heads turning, looking away from my position at the stake to some distant point behind them. Shouts rise in the distance.

"Stop that man!"

"Throw up barricades."

"Fire!"

A volley of gunshots crack, and the crowd falls to the ground, scrambling to the edge of the square.

And that's when I see him.

Damien charges toward me on a magnificent white steed, a bow stretched taut, an arrow nocked on the string, the shaft on fire.

He isn't in shining armor. He wears nothing but the ink that covers his skin. Though his face looks like approaching death, he is my knight come to rescue me.

"Damien!" I scream, as if he can't see me, the main event, tied to the stake. "I'm here! I'm here!"

The Black Watch move wordlessly, assembling before me in a half perimeter, unslinging assault rifles from across their backs.

"Light the pyre!" my mother screams. "Forget the lashes! Light the pyre!"

The chief executioner rises to his feet and glances at the kindling on which I stand. The bundled twigs are dry and reek of gasoline. All it would take is one, and I'd light up faster than a birthday candle.

"Don't do this," I say. "You're on live television. The Prince of Edenvale is approaching. Do you think he'll end you quickly if you kill his wife and child?"

The executioner turns to face Damien. My prince's expression is thunderous.

"I'm sorry, Your Highness." The executioner removes a long blade from the scabbard at his hip.

Before I can scream, he drives the blade down my middle, expertly cutting the ties that bind me without leaving so much as a scratch on my clothing.

"Your kindness will not be forgotten," I gasp.

He nods and sprints away without another word, ducking the flying bullets.

"Juliet!" Damien calls. "Dive to your left."

I don't question my husband. I simply obey. And as I hit the ground I see him unleash his arrow, lighting the pyre. Although now only the empty stake burns.

He kicks the haunches of his stallion and drives him forward. The waiting Black Watch have two choices: back into the flames or get run down by four churning hooves.

All take the surprise third option—fleeing in all four directions.

"Your hand," he shouts.

I rise to my feet, throwing up my arm. He grabs it and tugs, swinging me off the ground and over the horse.

"Yah, Maximus!" he urges.

"After them!" Mother calls in the distance.

Floodlights illuminate us.

"Looks like we've got some company," Damien growls, wrapping a hand around my middle and locking me against his torso.

An armored Jeep appears out of nowhere, the distance between it and us growing smaller by the second.

"Turn right!" I yell, and my heart warms as Damien veers in the direction of my command without question.

Maximus leaps over a three-foot hedge, and the Jeep slams to a screeching halt.

"Where are you taking us, Princess?"

"This is the way that I sneaked out the night we met at the Veil," I say. "The mountain on this side forms a natural barrier, but there is an old irrigation tunnel at the south corner that will bring us into the city."

"There," he says, driving the horse on.

The black mouth of the cave emerges from the night's shadows, and we tear into it, the horse not balking despite the fact that there are only inches of space on either side of us and maybe half a foot at best overhead. The light in the distance gets closer and closer with every one of Maximus's strides.

Then we burst out into the city, and four police cars career up the street, sirens blazing.

Damien veers the horse up an embankment and onto a steep road. "Do you remember where we are?" he says into my ear, his breath warm against my skin.

It takes me a minute before I realize where we are going. It's the same road we took when we left The Veil.

"We're going to Lovers' Leap," I gasp, craning my head around my shoulder so that I can meet his gaze. "Do you remember now?"

"Yes. I remember everything," he says, and his eyes burn. "Every last damn wonderful thing."

A sob wells in my throat. Even though we are racing for our lives, it's as if time has utterly stopped.

"I am going to get you out of here alive, and we are going to have our child and grow old somewhere safe and boring."

I burst out laughing. "Life with you will never be boring."

And then we're outside the city proper, retracing our path along the mountain's winding road until we're there. The Lovers' Leap.

For several seconds it's quiet, and I truly think we've outmaneuvered our pursuers.

But then there it is, the wail of the sirens as the four police cars skid around the corner.

"Do it," I say. "Go over the edge." My laugh is high and nervous. "Perhaps ours will have a happier ending."

Damien squeezes me tight. "There's no other way." His voice is tight.

"I trust you with my life," I answer with conviction. "And the life of our unborn child. Damien... I love you."

He kisses me short and sweet, his lips tasting like the promise of forever even if it only lasts for a moment.

And then, we leap.

CHAPTER EIGHTEEN

Damien

I SQUEEZE MY eyes shut and pull Juliet close. I will not let go of her. Even if our bodies lie broken at the base of this cliff, my wife will be in my arms. And at the very least, she will die knowing what I could not tell her before now.

"I love you, too!" I shout against the wind.

Then I feel weightless.

And then my teeth clatter as we land hard—Juliet, me and Maximus.

But we're still on the horse. And we're not dead.

"Are we dead?" Juliet asks.

"No," I say. "At least, I don't think so. Are you okay?"

"Yes."

Her voice carries in the eerie silence. It's so goddamn dark I don't know where we've landed. What I do know is that somewhere above us, flashlights shine down. But they don't reach our landing point. Hopefully, according to the guards above, our bodies are splattered way below. By the time they look for us at daybreak, perhaps they'll think our remains were collected by Edenvale.

I pat Maximus on the side. "Good job, boy."

He whimpers, and I feel him try to take a step but falter.

"Shit," I hiss.

"What is it?" Juliet whispers.

"That was a hard landing," I say. "On this night alone I've seen Maximus do things no horse should be able to do, but that fall?"

The ground beneath us shakes, and Juliet yelps.

"What's happening?" she cries.

I don't want to answer. Because logic says we've landed on a small outcropping—and that the weight of our impact has loosed the land from its precarious hold.

It appears this was only a short reprieve before the end.

Again we jerk, but there is still ground beneath us, and I don't feel the sensation of falling. In fact, it feels as if we're going backward.

We've landed on some sort of moving platform, which means whoever is at the end of it was waiting for us.

I reach for the bow and arrow, spinning toward Maximus's hindquarters and taking aim into the dark.

"It's the Black Watch," Juliet says, voice shaking. "They must have tunnels inside the mountain. I never knew. Mother and Father never said. Damien, I'm so sorry."

I want to comfort her, but there's no time.

I can feel Maximus's breathing going unsteady,

feel him faltering where he stands. I just need light. Once I can see who our captors are, I'll fire off as many shots as I can before they take me.

"We will not die without a fight," I say through gritted teeth, and I realize at this moment that this is the one thing I've never done—fought for what I loved.

With Victoria, I ran.

When Nikolai practically disowned me, I ran.

When Father decided to make an example of me through banishment, I ran.

I never fought to make things better. I never fought for what I wanted. I just. Fucking. Ran.

Not today.

We jerk to a halt, and the sound of a mechanical door closing echoes behind us.

And then—light.

I pull on the bow's string as soon as a figure takes shape before me. It only takes seconds for my eyes to adjust, and when they do, I drop the bow and arrow to the floor.

That's when the last of my lost memories takes hold, one I didn't even know was missing until now.

"We're going to let you live," the guard from the penthouse had said to me months ago. "Because you're going to lead us straight to Queen Cordelia so we can do what should have been done decades ago."

Not dead. She's—not dead.

"Mother?" My voice shakes. I don't even recognize it. And though I've never met the woman before me, she has lived these past decades in photographs and shared memories of my brothers and father.

She sucks in a sharp breath, the gesture contradicting the form-fitting utility suit, combat boots and what looks like rappelling gear.

I slide off the horse and help Juliet down. As soon as both of us are standing, Maximus collapses.

Dammit. Dammit. Dammit. We did not make it this far for my partner in crime to give up his life.

"Hang in there, buddy," I say, stroking his mane.

Again a whimper.

I move closer to the woman only a few feet away— a woman I almost shot point-blank with an arrow.

A woman who should already be dead.

I grab her wrist as anger rips through me, and she doesn't so much as make a sound. I shove her sleeve up to her elbow and find what I knew would be there—the tattoo of a crow's feather.

"You're part of The Order?" I yell. "All these years I've blamed myself for your death, and instead you've been running around with some secret organization rather than ruling your kingdom alongside your king?"

"Damien," Juliet says softly, her hand gripping my forearm and gently tugging me free. "Maybe she has an explanation."

I spin toward Juliet, seething. "An explanation? For deserting her family? For letting her youngest son live with the guilt of taking her life just so he could be born? Do you know what kind of living that is, knowing every breath you inhale belongs to someone else? There is nothing she could say—"

"I wasn't always part of The Order," she interrupts. "In fact, I was born on a farm a stone's throw from the very cliff you jumped from, the Lovers' Leap."

I shake my head. "The late queen of Edenvale was not Nightgardin born," I tell her, even as the slight accent in her voice registers.

"Come now, Damien," she says. "If you're going to be the ones to unite our two countries at last, I suggest you stop trying to explain away the obvious. Because you've already figured it out."

She's right. I am trying to explain away the obvious.

"You were Black Watch," I say.

She smiles. "Very good."

"Sent to kill Father," I add.

She nods. "But I failed my mission, and instead of ending Nikolai's life, I fell in love with him and bore him three sons. Three strong heirs. It was when the Watch started threatening my children that I knew something had to be done. At the time I had found I was pregnant with Damien—and I'd also recently found out about The Order."

"X," I say.

"Yes. He was so young when we met. Younger than me, yet already one of the most influential members. While his origin is still a mystery, I do know that he is the only agent of The Order raised in the organization since he was a teen. He brought me in, helped me stage my death, and in these past decades I've risen in the ranks to European director. But now, Damien. Now I can come home thanks to you and Juliet."

"I don't understand," Juliet says, breaking her silence. "My country wants me dead."

My mother grins and shakes her head. "Your crazy mother wants you dead. Pity she's forgotten how little power women in royalty truly have in this country if they are not supported by their king."

It's then that another figure appears, one I realize now was absent from the melee in the square.

"Oh my God," Juliet says. "Father."

Juliet

"Daughter." My formal, distant father steps forward, wrapping me in a giant bear hug. "Thank God. I thought I'd lost you for good tonight."

"You mean this wasn't what you wanted?" I ask. "Where were you? Why didn't you help me?"

A dark look crossed his features. "She drugged me."

"Mother?"

He nods once. "She has been for weeks. I've only now learned the truth. She's spread rumors of me taking ill when it's been all her, keeping me bedridden and docile in the palace while she set her plans in motion."

Damien's mother steps forward, the same woman who questioned me in The Hole. "We rescued him two hours ago. Once we were able to administer an infusion to counteract his sedatives, he returned to full health and full mental capacity."

"And now we will put an end to my wife's mad ambitions," he says. "For too long I haven't taken her words seriously. All her talk about finding Edenvale's hidden Spring of Youth, of wanting to rule forever. At first, years ago when she started speaking of such things, I thought they were silly daydreams. But then came the daily injections, the plastic surgeries, these strange longevity diets. Finally, when I realized she truly thought she could rule eternally, I told her she was raving, that perhaps she needed psychiatric care. That's when I conveniently took ill, and from there on out, she's been coming into my chambers every six hours to keep me in a stupor while putting out official word that I was sick. There's no time to lose now. Nightgardin needs a king tonight."

"And Edenvale will come to your aid," Damien says, glancing to his mother. "You still have much to explain, Mother, but tonight we will destroy the monster who threatens my family and create a safe future for my wife and child."

"Damien." His mother's voice is husky, and I'm struck by how similar they look in manner and expression. "I am so proud of the man you've become—and the father you will soon be."

"Speaking of fathers…" He gazes at her with an intense expression. "Tell me this one thing, does the king know that you still live?"

A look of raw pain cuts the grooves of her face. "No. He has no idea. I couldn't put him in danger. I sacrificed everything I love for my family, and I don't regret or apologize for that choice."

"Not even when he remarried our stepmother?"

Her shoulders stiffen. "He couldn't be expected to live like a monk."

"But…" Realization dawns on me. "Your Highness. Queen Cordelia. You are the lawful queen. You have to tell King Nikolai the truth."

A small muscle twitches in her jaw. "He'll never understand. While I have loved him all these years, I don't expect he has done the same. And I don't think

I can bear to have him look at me with the hate or anger or betrayal I know he will feel once he learns the truth."

Damien laces his fingers through mine and pulls me closer, planting a kiss on the top of my head. "Trust me, Mother, if there is one thing that I've learned, it's that love works in mysterious ways. I cannot promise he will forgive you. But if you do not give him—and your sons—the chance to know the whole truth, how can we see your deception as anything other than a betrayal?"

Queen Cordelia nods, her piercing eyes glossy with the threat of tears, eyes so like my husband's. "We shall see. But for now, we need to focus. The mission is to get into Nightgardin Palace and allow the king to gain control the situation."

"And how will we do that?" I ask. "Mother's not going to go without a fight."

"What did I miss?" X appears, zipping up his tactical vest.

"You're here too." Last I knew, he was taking the fake doctor to The Hole.

X smirks, tapping his earpiece. "I've been listening to events unfold in real time. The helicopter is on standby. It's time to strike hard and fast."

I arch a brow. "Don't you ever drive a car like a normal person?"

"I'm an excellent driver." He gives me a cryptic wink.

"Good luck, my son. I will be here, too, inside your ear." The queen hands Damien an earpiece microphone. "We have eyes in the palace. Follow my orders, and we'll be reunited by sunrise."

"And you will then come back to Edenvale with me, and see my father? My brothers?" My husband is nothing if not persistent.

She shuffles her feet, her features locking into an unsettled expression. "Yes. It is time. I only hope that…" She draws a shaky breath and forces a smile. "The next twelve hours shall be most interesting."

"And Maximus," I ask worriedly. The stallion rests behind us, trying to appear brave, but from the way his large nostrils flare, it's obvious he is in incredible pain, pain he endures for saving our life. "What will happen to him? I think his leg is broken."

The queen squares her shoulders. "He saved your life, and the life of my son and grandchild. I'll personally ensure that he receives the best vet care that money can buy and a long retirement in a meadow filled with clover."

X turns to us. "Time to fly."

X expertly lands the stealth helicopter in the southern corner of the palace grounds.

"Princess, would you like to remain here? It will be safest," he says as Damien helps Father leap four feet to the ground.

"Not a chance," I say, jumping too. "My body might be bruised, but there's no way I'm going to let you boys have all the fun. After what my mother has done to me—to Damien's family—I want to make sure she is stopped for good. And I want my face to be the last she sees before she is imprisoned—or killed."

An owl hoots, and X cups a hand to his mouth and returns the eerie call.

"That's a good sign," he says with satisfaction.

"What does it mean?" Damien asks.

"The Order is assembled at their positions throughout the castle. Right now they are locking your mother in the throne room and laying siege to those members of the Black Watch who pledged loyalty to the queen."

"They shall pay for their treachery," my father growls.

"Soon," I say, placing a hand on his arm. "We will make sure they are locked away and can never threaten the peace here in this realm again."

Father's eyes grow misty. "I've made so many mistakes with you, Juliet," he says. "But once I've made the way clear for you, I'd like nothing better than to abdicate, allowing you to bring Nightgardin into the twenty-first century alongside your husband."

"Oh, Papa!" I cry, throwing myself at him.

"Let's roll," X says.

Damien reaches out and extends his arm. "Princess, are you ready to take back your kingdom?"

"With you by my side? Absolutely." I grin and place my hand on his elbow. "Are you ready to become a king?"

He brushes his lips on my temple. "I've always thought I'm not worthy of anything other than a lifetime of banishment and regret. But meeting you has changed everything, Juliet. I know now that with you, anything is possible."

"Then let's not wait another minute," I say, and we race toward our future.

CHAPTER NINETEEN

Damien

WHEN WE REACH the throne room, I move to enter, but X places a hand on my shoulder and nods toward Juliet.

"Is it safe?" I ask him.

"Yes, Your Highness," he answers with a clipped bow.

I take a step back.

"This is your palace," I tell my wife, gesturing her forward. "Claim it."

She laces her fingers through mine and shakes her head.

"It is ours now, my king. We will take it together."

So we enter, hand in hand, to find a host of bodies on the floor—those who resisted The Order. Then there are those members of the Black Watch who surrendered, bound and guarded by X and my mother's comrades. But what stands out among all of it is the Nightgardin queen herself, still sitting regally on her throne, a glass of wine in her hand.

"Bravo, daughter," she purrs, laying eyes on Juliet.

"It seems you've won, but I will not surrender. If I cannot rule, then this ends on my terms."

She raises the glass to her lips, and before it even registers what she's about to do, a feral cry comes from behind.

"No! No poison!" Juliet's father cries, and then I hear the whistle of an arrow sail past.

The crystal goblet falls, shattering on the flagstones. The queen screams as the arrow impales her forearm, pinning it to the back of the throne.

Blood streams from the wound as the king stalks toward his wife, bow still in hand.

"Death is not the answer," he roars at her. "You need help, my love."

She shakes her head as she writhes from what must be unbearable pain.

"I will not grow old," she cries through gritted teeth as the king approaches. "I will not live out my days behind the bars of a dusty cell!"

He drops the bow when he reaches the dais, and the whole room looks on in wonder as he pulls a blade from his pocket, cuts off the shaft of the arrow, and pulls it gingerly from her arm.

The queen wails and then blacks out.

"Did you know your father was such a marksman?" I whisper to Juliet.

She shakes her head, her dark eyes wide as she takes in the scene before her. "I knew he practiced archery, but Mother never permitted me to join him at the range."

The king turns to face his audience.

"The queen must answer for her crimes against our country—against her own daughter and husband," he says. "But death is not the answer. Not when she can still be helped. She will be locked away. Of that I promise you. But she will be given the medical care she needs to bring back the woman I once loved." He drops to one knee. "Allow me this last pardon as I abdicate the throne to you—Queen Juliet and King Damien. May you rule as you see fit, as equals. And may you bring together two countries that have brutally battled for far too long." He bows his head. "I humbly request that I be allowed to retire to a monastery to live out the rest of my days in contemplation and prayer. I have much to atone for."

I squeeze Juliet's hand. "This is your call, my queen. I follow your lead."

Juliet squeezes back but does not release her firm grip. She is nervous, but I also know she is so very strong.

She squares her shoulders and holds her head high. "Thank you, Father," she says, voice steady. "I will show mercy on my queen mother. We will set a date for her trial when she has recovered from her wound."

Juliet's father stands and scoops her still-unconscious mother into his arms.

"Thank you, Your Highness," he says, bowing his head once more. Then he is escorted from the room by three members of the Order.

It is then that I see him, bound and gagged by another member—the guard of the Watch who dragged Juliet from my penthouse the weekend they stole my memories. The same guard who took her from me again at the hospital, leaving me bleeding on an elevator floor.

"I wish I could say I shared your penchant for mercy," I say to my wife. "Perhaps someday you can teach me."

And then I let go of her hand and stalk toward the guard.

I untie his gag, and he spits it from his mouth.

"What did she promise you?" I seethe.

The man says nothing.

I lift his bound hands, examining the scars on the right one—the one my wife bit as she was brutally dragged back to her murderous mother by this man. The man who then let his compatriots beat me to within inches of my own life. The man responsible for Juliet's almost dying tonight.

I note his square jaw, the perfect slope of his nose, his clean-shaven, unblemished skin.

"She promised you eternal life. Didn't she?" I ask, amused. "She promised you'd be the perfect specimen you are right now forever, did she not?"

He makes a move to wrap his bound hands around my neck, but he is too slow. I block him with one hand, then punch him in the face with the other.

Bone crunches against my fist, and blood pours from his nose, covering his lips and neck. He screams, and I shake out my hand, every one of my knuckles split and bleeding. But damn it was worth it.

"See that the wound is not properly set," I say.

"Yes, Your Highness, King Damien."

The answer comes in unison from from the brothers and sisters of The Order—X included. The words even echo in my earpiece, ringing loud and clear in my mother's voice.

"And make sure that whatever cell he is locked in until his trial has mirrors on every wall so he can never escape looking at his ruined face."

I run fingers over the scars on my own face, old and new, and for the first time in years I do not dwell on how much I deserve each one—on how many people in my life I have let down. Instead, they remind me how far I've come, that I have earned my brother's forgiveness and the love of my wife. My queen.

I make my way to Juliet and wrap my arms around her, pulling her to me so tightly.

She squeezes just as hard, and I know it's all hitting her, too—all the steps it took to get us here.

"Sorry about that," I say. "But he hurt you, and I couldn't let that go."

Juliet shrugs. "If you hadn't broken his nose, I might have had to bite him again. You saved me the trouble."

I laugh, then rest a hand on her belly where our unborn child still lives and grows, and I know now the depth of love a mother or father is capable of.

I know that despite her betrayal, my mother did what she had to do to protect us all.

Hand in hand, Juliet and I stride toward the dais. Then we turn to face the crowd before she takes a seat in one throne, and I in the other.

"I forgive you, Mother," I say quietly, knowing she is listening in. "It's time for you to come home."

Juliet

This arrival to Edenvale Palace is very different to my first. For one thing, we are traveling in a motorcade, an honor befitting a prince…and a to-be-annointed-queen.

"It's going to be okay," Damien tells his mother for the tenth time in as many minutes.

I take an opportunity to study her pale face, her bloodless lips. She is still beautiful, although her years in isolation have marked deep grooves near her eyes.

Her penetrating gaze flits to me, and not for the first time do I marvel at the resemblance between her and her son.

"Why do you watch me so?" she asks.

I swallow hard, unnerved by her forthrightness but also appreciating that from now on I'll be living among people who demand honesty in all dealings. "I admire you."

Her delicate nostrils flare in surprise.

"You sacrificed everything to keep your children safe." I place a hand on my belly. "In not that many months, I'm going to bear my own child, and I can only hope that if the time ever came to make such a difficult decision, I'd be half as selfless as you."

She answers with a soft smile. "Something tells me, Juliet, that you will be a fierce and remarkable queen."

As we speed through the open front gates of the castle, a long line of guards lift brass trumpets to their lips and begin playing Edenvale's national anthem.

On the front steps stand Nikolai and Benedict, Kate and Evangeline…and Damien's father. The king.

Damien steps out and helps his mother and then me from the Rolls-Royce.

The trumpets finish their song and silence reigns.

King Nikolai practically stumbles down the steps leading to the circle drive. "C-Cordelia?" he stammers, the first time that I've ever heard the regal man speak with anything but perfect eloquence. "Dear God, is it really you? They told me you were coming, but I swore it was an imposter, some publicity trick. I didn't dare let my heart hope."

"You—hoped. Oh, Niki," Queen Cordelia sobs, and just like that the king sprints across the gap separating them and draws his wife into his arms, claiming her in a passionate kiss that practically sends up a plume of steam.

"I'll still be kissing you like that when we're their age, you know," Damien growls into my ear, nipping my earlobe. "But right now, all I want to do is get you inside."

I shiver, knowing exactly what he means. The tension between us is electric, and as much as I want to focus on the happy reunion playing out on the front steps as Cordelia embraces both of her two other sons, I can't ignore the ache between my legs. An ache that begs for Damien to be inside me like we were those months ago—like we were meant to be. I am no longer a bewildered girl shameful of my sexual urges, but a queen ready to claim what is rightfully mine.

"We're going inside to clean ourselves," Damien announces, and I try to ignore X's chuckle.

As we walk away, the king calls out, "Wait, my son. A word."

Damien stiffens beside me. "Father?"

"Thank you." The king's eyes mist over. "You have given me back my soul. I can never make up for the years of our estrangement, but I want you to know that I'll work hard to repair the rift between us."

"As will I," Benedict adds.

"And I." Nikolai steps forward and shakes his brother's hand. "You have set our family on a course for a future even brighter than I dared to hope. Thank you on behalf of the kingdom and from me, your brother."

They both aggressively clear their throats and clap each other's shoulders.

Then we make it up to our chamber. How we get there I do not know. Perhaps we float, because it doesn't seem possible that we could have walked a single step. All I know is that here we are, naked, kneeling before each other in the middle of the king-size bed, fitting for Damien's new role as King of Nightgardin. My home, which is now ours.

His hand works between my legs. It's not as if I need to be primed for him, but I relish the attention of his clever fingers on my swollen clit.

He groans as I lick my palm and work his shaft from root to tip. Soon that thick head will be inside me. My mouth waters in anticipation.

"Are you nervous?" he asks.

"No, my love," I croon in a husky voice.

He barks a short laugh. "That makes one of us."

I grab his wrist as he attempts to thrust two fingers into my aching heat. "No. I need you. Just you."

"Juliet," he grinds out, pushing me onto the bed. "I'm not sure I can be gentle."

"Good." I rake my nails down his muscular back as he roars. "Because I want the full Damien experience."

He dips down and gives one of my nipples a punishing suck that sends me bowing off the bed. "Careful what you wish for," he says.

With a rock of his hips, his length glides inside me, filling me not only between my legs, but into my very heart. I wrap my thighs around his trim hips and undulate my body in time with his rhythm. He adjusts the angle, ensuring his pelvis grinds me right where I need him. Our lips meet, demanding, plundering, claiming. It will take two strong people to heal the ravages of the Nightgardin monarchy, but together we set a course for a new regime—a future unlike I ever could have imagined.

"Damien," I gasp, feeling my climax roll over me like an inexorable wave. "I love you. I love you so much."

"I love you beyond the power of speech," he says. "You saved me, in so many more ways than you could ever imagine."

"We saved each other," I tell him, because it is the complete and utter truth.

"My queen." He heaves against me as we shatter in unison.

And I know then that we are no royal mess, that our future together is nothing short of beautiful.

EPILOGUE

Damien

JULIET AND I head to Edenvale for our monthly family dinner. If it weren't for the grand dining room—along with the fact that said room is inside a palace—I'd swear we were your average family. One who laughs together, dines together and is so full of love.

And comprises two queens, kings, princes and princesses who sometimes participate in high-speed chases while foiling plots to steal water from a supposed spring of youth.

"X," I say, and he looks up from where he butters a roll on his plate. Ever since Mother's homecoming, he has been our guest rather than our employee. But tonight is his last night with us, which is why—even though Juliet is in her final weeks of pregnancy—she insisted we come.

So much has happened in the past several months that it seems we've all but forgotten what started it all. I've been waiting for X to offer the information on his own, but he has not. Perhaps it is because he is charged with guarding the secret, but I think we've all earned the right to know.

After X is reassigned, who knows if we will see him again?

"Yes, Your Highness?"

"Is the spring real?"

The room goes silent, and everyone's eyes volley between me and X.

He nods once. "It is, but it is not as you think."

"Hundreds of years ago," my mother begins, "a great plague swept through our lands—from here all the way to Nightgardin. Miners in Edenvale had been carving out the catacombs for decades after the last great war, and they came upon an underground waterfall that ended in a small pool, so—not exactly a spring." She winks. "Thinking it nothing but an unknown water source, they drank from it as they worked—with permission of the royal family, of course, so long as they hauled buckets of it to the palace to store in case of drought."

She nods toward X.

"Wives and children of the miners took ill with the plague," he said. "And died quickly. But the miners who drank from the spring not only survived, they lived longer and stayed healthier than any other in the land—as did your ancestors." He glances toward me and my brothers.

"Nightgardin learned of the spring," I said.

My mother nods. "But by the time word reached them, the story had been twisted into a myth, one that they believed."

"And that has been the source of our differences for all these years?" I ask.

X nods. "And The Order has kept it protected and hidden all this time." His gaze trails toward a por-

trait on the far wall—one of my father sitting alone
on his throne—one Evangeline painted not too long
ago. "The map is safely hidden as well," he says.
"Should you ever choose to find it and see if its waters still run deep."

"Oh!" Juliet's goblet of water topples forward,
soaking the table as she stands with a start.

"What is it?" I ask.

She grips her round belly with one hand while
the other braces against the table. "Contraction," she
says. "And I think—my water just broke."

Across the table, Kate yelps and grips Nikolai's
arm.

"Good Lord, you have to be kidding me," he says.
"You're four weeks early!"

"And I'm two weeks early," Juliet says through labored breaths. "But it looks like there are two babies
coming tonight!"

In mere minutes we are at the royal hangar. X hops
in the Rolls with my parents, Benedict and Evangeline, ready to lead our small entourage through the
city. Nikolai tosses me the keys to an SUV.

"You sure?" I ask him.

"There's no one I trust more to get us there fast
and safe."

"No trusty white steed?" Juliet asks when her contraction subsides.

I grin. "Not tonight, love. While he's healing well,
Maximus isn't quite ready for a ride of this importance. But by the time our little one is able to ride, I
will trust no one but him for her training."

As we come to a halt in front of the emergency

care doors, I see my parents along with Benedict and Evangeline already bursting through the entrance.

Juliet has another contraction, and I turn my attention to her for the fifteen seconds it takes her to get through it.

When I look back to where X was standing, he is gone.

Nikolai claps me on the shoulder. "Ready to meet your daughter?" he says with a grin.

"Ready to meet your son?" I answer.

I throw open the door and hop down, sprinting to Juliet's side of the car.

"Are you ready?" I ask her.

She bites her lip and nods.

My eyes widen. "Wait! I almost forgot." I pull the diamond ring from my pocket and kneel down beside her door.

"We never quite did this part. I'd planned something for when we got home tonight, but—"

"Put that ring on my finger and get me inside!" she yells, but the most glorious smile takes over her features.

I do as I'm told and scoop her into my arms. She laughs. "I love you, my strong, courageous, beautiful queen."

She wraps her hands around my neck. "I love you, too. Now let's go meet our future."

I carry her through the doors.

For so many years I thought my life was about making it to the finish line, but now I realize I don't ever want this race to end. In fact, I think I'm finally ready to slow down and just enjoy the ride.

X

I CHECK THE Rolex on my wrist as I stalk from the hospital. The new royal driver appointed by the Order will be here shortly to escort all those not giving birth back to the palace following the birth of the new heirs.

The moment is bittersweet. My time with the Lorentz family has come to a close with this new reassignment. I'm not one for goodbyes, so I made an unceremonious exit on the pretext of fetching Princess Kate ice chips and sent a nurse back with the disposable cup instead.

The unmarked black sedan idles outside the main entrance. I hesitate before climbing into the back seat. I'm not used to being the one driven.

The door pops open. Someone is impatient for my arrival.

A slender arm covered in a long satin glove emerges, a blindfold dangling from her index finger.

"You know the rules, X," the woman purrs. "No revealing of identities. Just the pleasure of the ride."

I know she's already wearing hers, so I grab the

small garment and affix it over my eyes, then feel my way into the vehicle.

"It's been a few months," she says.

My hand travels in her direction, my fingertips brushing a bare thigh.

"It's good to see you, Z."

I slide my hand up her leg and under her skirt and feel her knees fall open.

No panties.

She sucks in a breath as I slide one finger into her slick warmth.

"Do you ever wonder what I look like?" she asks.

I grin and lean toward her, using the sound of her voice to find my way to her lips. I nip at her bottom one.

"Does it matter?" I ask.

We've never truly met each other. For as long as I've known of her, she's been working for the East Asian Order. We connected via missions online, but both know the futility of anything other than a physical relationship. To get attached is to endanger one's lover. And so, we do this.

"Do you want to?" she asks, and I pump my finger inside her. She writhes against my palm.

It's fun. It's fast. And above all no strings, just how I like it.

I'll risk everything, except my heart.

"Time for a taste," I say, then drop to my knees in the spacious back seat and drink my fill.

She digs her fingers into my hair and cries out.

I'll make us both forget the question of intimacy. Hell, I'll make her forget her own name.

This is all I allow myself to want, these short interludes with a woman whose face I've never seen and never will.

Nothing more.

* * * * *

COMING SOON!

We really hope you enjoyed reading this book. If you're looking for more romance, be sure to head to the shops when new books are available on

Thursday
4th October

LET'S TALK
Romance

For exclusive extracts, competitions
and special offers, find us online:

f facebook.com/millsandboon

◉ @millsandboonuk

▼ @millsandboon

Or get in touch on 0844 844 1351*

For all the latest titles coming soon, visit
millsandboon.co.uk/nextmonth